AMY'S BIG BREAK

Linsey J Cross

For permission requests, please contact:
linseyjcross@yahoo.co.uk
https://www.facebook.com/linseyjcross/

Editorial services by www.bookeditingservices.co.uk

For Mel
For the sunshine and cocktails we missed out on this year

CONTENTS

CHAPTER ONE

I sit up to turn off my alarm and hear rain pattering against the window. Another dreary April in Damsbury. The clock is flashing 6:25 a.m. I drag myself out of bed and try to find something I can wear for work that doesn't require ironing. I really ought to start getting more organised, but still living with my parents, I prefer to just head straight to my bedroom once I get in from work to have my own space. I manage to find a stripy Warehouse dress; that'll do nicely. With a blast of dry shampoo in my hair and some minimal make-up applied, I'm ready to go. I like to get in early on a Friday so I can leave early.

I go into the kitchen and see Dad sitting at the table having his toast and reading the newspaper. Mum is standing at the counter making them both a cuppa.

'Morning, morning! Late, late, late!' I mumble as I open the fridge. I grab a yoghurt and shove it into my handbag.

'Morning, love!' they both chime in unison. Oh to be retired, it must be bliss! Why on earth they get up so early when they don't need to is beyond me.

'Amy, will Danny be joining us for tea tonight?' Mum calls.

'Er...not sure yet, Mum. Might be meeting him at the pub. I'll let you know later?' I grumble, opening the front door. Mum loves Danny; Dad, I think, just tolerates him for me. But who is ever going to be good enough for a daddy's little girl really?

'OK, have nice day at work, dear,' Mum shouts out as I close the door behind me. I scramble to the car, juggling my bag and keys, trying to not get too drenched.

I run into the office, as quick as my stilettos will let me, whilst holding my handbag over my head to try and avoid getting my hair wet. When I reach my desk and switch on the computer, I pull my phone out of my bag. Time to text Danny: *Morning babe, just got to work. Are we still meeting for a drink later? Miss you xx.* I look forward to seeing Danny all week. He works in London and stays there during the week, so I only get to see him at the weekends. Monday to Thursday is so rubbish, at work all day, home with my parents all evening – I feel more in my happy place at the weekends in Danny's flat. I appreciate Mum asking him for dinner, but I'd much rather go back to Danny's, where we can chill out in our own environment.

My boss storms into the office, breaking my daydream. She's shouting into her hands-free headset, looking immaculate as always. She shakes out her umbrella and puts it in the stand. She turns to face me whilst making great hand gestures and rolling her eyes. She shouts goodbye at whoever's on the phone and starts strutting towards my desk.

'Morning, Amy!' she squeals. She's always so happy.

'Good Morning, Lauren.'

'You wouldn't believe the day I'm having already, and I've not even had my morning caffeine fix yet. Would you be a darling and fetch me a coffee? Then I need you to forget whatever you were doing today. I have a heap of data I need you to compile, and we need to get it to procurement by close of play today!'

'Sure, whatever you need, boss!'

'Great, thanks, Amy, you're a superstar. Go fetch us some caffeine, and I'll run through what I need you to do. Here, use my card.' She hands me her platinum credit card.

I do like Lauren, but I'm not gonna lie, I'm a little envious of her too. She is stunningly beautiful and has the best wardrobe a girl could wish for. Oh, and she's rich. Daddy owns the company. Stevenson & Co. She is a great boss to work for, though. She lets me leave early whenever I want, doesn't complain if I'm late and treats me to posh coffee all the time! I guess that's what's keeping me in this dead-end job, if I'm honest. There's no position I can transfer to, unless someone leaves or retires. I'm twenty-six and still living with my parents, which is not ideal! I wouldn't ever be able to afford a place on my own.

Part of me is hoping that Danny will ask me to move in with him. He's not even there all week; it's not as though it would make any difference to his life now. We've been together for four years, yet he doesn't ever seem to want to take our relationship to the next level.

I enter the coffee shop and order Lauren's Americano and my skinny latte, and I can't help but order a croissant, which is the size of my face. I was going to be so good and just have a yoghurt for breakfast. Diet be damned! I pull my phone out my bag, Danny has replied: *Sure Ames, meet you in The Bull after work xx.* My heart skips a beat…roll on 5:30 p.m.

By the time I get to the pub, I look like a drowned rat. I head straight for the ladies to tart myself up the best I can with the contents of my handbag. I spritz my long curly brown hair with my de-frizzing spray and scrunch it underneath the hand dryer. I wipe the black mascara patches from under my eyes, spread on some lip gloss and shower myself in perfume. There, five-minute makeover complete!

I head to the bar and see that Danny has already ordered a glass of white wine for me. He's leaning against the bar, still in his work suit, which makes him look hot! I do love a man in a suit.

'Hi, babe,' I say, beaming at him before giving the biggest hug.

'Hi, Ames,' he replies. I notice that his arms are limp around me. Something's wrong.

'You OK?' I ask, grabbing my drink.

'Yeah, fine. Let's go sit at a table.' He picks up his drink and leads us over to the corner of the pub.

'How's your week been?' I sit next to him and rest my hand on his knee.

'OK,' he answers.

My phone beeps. I pull it out of my bag and see that it's a text from Mum. 'Oh, Mum wants to know if you want tea at ours tonight?' I ask as I start tapping out a reply.

'No, not tonight. Tell her thanks, though.'

As I finish writing my reply, he's up getting another pint already. Blimey, he drank that quickly. Something doesn't seem right; he seems quiet. I feel as though I always have to make the effort lately. He's hard to have a conversation with and I'm always texting him first. He's probably just busy with his important London job, I tell myself.

He comes back to the table, and I take a sip of my wine, it's cold and crisp down my throat.

'You're drinking fast tonight. Everything OK at work?' I ask, placing my hand on his knee again.

'Yeah, work's fine,' he replies. And we sit there in silence for a bit.

'Wanna get a takeout tonight?' I ask.

'Maybe.' Well, this is hard work.

'OK, well, we can decide later. Any good films on tonight?' I ask, stretching for conversation. He's probably just tired.

'Dunno,' he mutters. Then he takes my hand off his knee and turns to face me. 'Look, there is something I need to talk to you about, Amy, and I needed a bit of Dutch courage before I could say it, because it's not going to be very nice.'

'What's up?' I try to keep my voice light while my mind is racing wondering what's going on.

He looks at me and ruffles his short brown hair, his brown eyes looking deep into mine. 'I'm not sure how to begin.' He starts to fidget and looks everywhere but at me.

'Danny, tell me what's going on.' I reach for his hand to try and steady it in mine, but he pulls away.

'Look, Ames, things haven't really been going anywhere with us for a while now...'

My heart sinks. 'What do you mean? I thought things were great?'

'Amy, you can't honestly think that. I feel like we've been drifting apart for a while, and I'm in London so much... I just think it's time for us to end this. I'm going to sell my flat and move there permanently.'

'Well, I can move with you! My job here is crappy anyway. I can come with you and get a job in London! I'm sure it won't be that hard! We can't just throw four years away!' I realise at this point I have tears streaming down my cheeks and people are starting to stare at us. I look at Danny as he's rubbing his head.

He looks me straight in the eyes and says, 'You don't get it, do you, Amy? There's…there's someone else.'

His words cut me like a knife; I'm uncontrollably sobbing now. '*Who? How long has it been going on? Is she from London? Do you love her?*' I don't think I honestly want the answers to all these questions, but they're just flying out of my mouth.

He looks down at the floor now, unable to look me in the eye any longer. 'Yes, I work with her… It's been for a while now. And, yes, I think I love her.'

'THINK!' I spit out. 'You *think* you love her? You either do or you don't! Do you still love *me*?' I know I sound desperate. I thought I was a strong woman, but I did not see this coming. It's knocked me for six.

'Well, I *thought* I loved you, but now I know I didn't. And now I *think* I love her. I'm sorry, Ames, I never meant to hurt you, but I met this woman at work and she's amazing, and I never knew I could feel like this about anyone. So yes, I *thought* I loved you, but I think I've only recently learnt what love is.'

I feel like I've just been punched in the gut. I double over and realise I'm breathing rapidly.

'I'm so sorry, Amy. I didn't want to hurt you.'

'Stop it! I don't…want to…hear…any…more!' I scream in between sobs. I straighten up, take a breath, pick up my wine and throw it in his face! 'You absolute shitbag!' He just sits there with a shocked look on his face. To be honest, I'm quite shocked myself!

Feeling as though I've regained some dignity, I grab my bag, storm out of the pub and straight into the rain. The rain actually feels good and refreshing on my hot, clammy skin, and it's calming away my tears. How did I have no idea what was going on? I feel so stupid! I pull my phone out; I need to ring my bestie. I manage to find Stephanie's number through my blurry vision and the rain splats falling onto my screen and press the call button.

She answers on the second ring. 'Hi, Ames!'

'Steph,' I sob, 'I need a drink!'

'Amy, what's the matter?'

'It's Danny... We've broke up!'

'OMG! What happened? Babe, I'm in town with some of the guys from work. Wanna come join? You can tell me all about it while we get hammered!'

'Yes please, that sounds great. I need to go home first. I'm a mess!' Actually, it doesn't sound all that great, but it sounds better than sitting at home with Mum and Dad all night.

'Right, get home, get yourself glammed up, and get ya ass here! Don't take too long, though, coz I'm already three drinks and one shot in, so you already have some catching up to do!'

Just hearing her voice makes me feel better. 'I won't be long. Where are you?'

'JJ's, of course! Where else can you dance the night away in this crappy town? Get your ass here ASAP and stop blubbering over that knobhead!'

I put the phone down and smile as I walk the last few steps home. Steph will make everything better – she always does. We've been best friends since we met in senior school. Clubbing is totally not what I feel like doing right now. But I need Steph, and I need a drink. And the last thing I need is to be stuck in with my mum and dad whilst crying over a boy. I love them both dearly, but I'm not going to sit with them and discuss boy stuff. My phone bleeps in my hand. A text from Steph: *Got you a shot in, babe. Hurry up so I can give you a hug! ☹ xxx.* I walk into the house and run straight for my room. Time to go and attempt to get 'glammed up'.

◆ ◆ ◆

I text Steph to let her know I'm here just as the taxi pulls up outside JJ's, as I don't want to walk in on my own.

Steph bumbles out of the doorway looking slightly tipsy and screams out, 'AMES! BABES!' She yanks open the taxi door, throws a £20 note at the driver and drags me out. 'Here you go, mate, keep the change!' As she pulls me into the biggest hug, I start blubbering again. 'Oh no you don't! Did you put waterproof mascara on?'

I choke out a laugh. 'Yes!'

'Good. Come with me, hon, and tell me all about it.' She marches me straight into the ladies.

Sitting on the sink unit together, I replay the whole conversation, stopping when anyone comes over to use the sink – which isn't as often as it should be, actually. Who are these people who don't wash their hands? Ew! Unless the sight of me snivelling is putting them off their usual hygiene.

'Oh, babe, I can't believe he did that to you. What does he mean *thought* he loved you and *thinks* he loves her? What a div!' she says sympathetically whilst handing me tissues. 'Dab. Don't rub!' she orders. I do as she says and gently dab away the tears from my face.

'I suppose I should've seen it coming,' I say. 'It's not like we were going anywhere. I just… That's all I know… I live for my weekends with him… The rest of my life just seems so…dull!'

'Hey! You have fantastic nights out with me!' she yells whilst prodding me in the ribs.

'Yes!' I laugh. 'Of course I have fantastic nights out with you, when we get to see each other!'

'And you'll be able to come out with me more now you're not saving your weekends for him!' says Steph.

She has a point. Steph works hard all week and plays hard all weekend, so I rarely get to see her. She's always working late, then at weekends I see Danny. She turns into a party animal every weekend, and I'm usually sat in with Danny watching some crappy sci-fi movie I don't even like, just because it means

I get to see him.

Steph jumps down from the sink and turns to face the mirror. 'Come on, time to sort out that blubbering face and go get drunk. I'm sobering up, and that is not good! I know it's early days, but there's a couple of cute guys from the office that have *Amy's rebound* written all over them!'

I laugh and jump down to look in the mirror. My God. My eyes are so puffy! Steph looks amazing – her long blonde hair smooth and straight, smokey eye make-up that makes her blue eyes pop, her neutral glossy lips. She's wearing the shortest denim skirt I think I've ever seen, with a black halterneck top and heels so high I don't know how she walks in them. She puts my two-and-a-half-inch stilettos to shame.

Looking at my reflection, I see a frumpy, drab, puffy-eyed person staring back at me. This is not who I used to be. I used to be like Steph: Bubbly and full of life. Slim and attractive. I'm wearing jeans and a vest top with a shirt half buttoned up over it. I look alright. I look smart...but I used to look better. I think about when Danny used to comment on my outfit if I was going out with Steph for the night: *'Don't you think that skirt's a bit short!'* or *'That top's a bit revealing, isn't it?'* I hadn't even noticed how my whole wardrobe had changed, until now. I reapply my lipstick and give my hair a quick shake.

'Ready, hon?' asks Steph.

'Ready.' I take a deep breath, link arms with her and we make our way towards the bar. I'm not sure what I've become, but I am determined I'm going to find me again.

A couple of hours later, I'm slurring quite a lot. I wonder if anyone else has noticed or if I'm getting away with it. All Steph's work friends are so nice, and they all have money. I don't think I've put my hand in my purse all night.

One of Steph's colleagues comes over with a tray full of shots. 'Jägerbombs!' he announces as he settles the tray in front of me.

'Woo! Thanks, Josh!' I say before picking one up and downing it before anyone else has even lifted theirs off the tray.

'John,' he corrects me. 'My name is John.'

I wave my hand. 'Yeah, whatever, they're *sooo* similar!'

Steph laughs, and I can hear her apologising to him on my behalf. Oops. I forgot she has to work with these people.

'The room is feeling spinny!' I slur at Steph as she grabs my arm and starts to drag me onto the dance floor.

'What you need, Ames, is to dance this off a little! Come on!' she says with a giggle. With that, we are on the dance floor.

As the next song begins, I feel somebody grinding up against me. It's not Steph; she's in front of me. What the…? I turn around and it's John. He pulls me closer, smiling and dancing in rhythm with me. This guy can dance! He's quite handsome too, in a rugged sort of way. He has a beard; I'd never usually go for anyone with a beard. But he is quite charming, and he is in a suit. Love a man in a suit. He's making eyes at me, which makes me think he's going to kiss me. Maybe I'm just imagining it because I'm wasted. I flirt and dance around him, hoping I look sexy and not like a drunk girl stumbling around barely keeping herself upright. Then he leans down to kiss me. I start off feeling like a goddess. YES! I still have it! That beard, though. It's quite off-putting. And it's not…it's not Danny. The kiss just feels all wrong. Then suddenly, I feel like I'm going to be sick. Uh-oh. I pull away and chuck up all over the dance floor, and John's shoes. Oops.

Steph quickly drags me into the loo, bends me over the toilet and holds back my hair. 'It's OK, babes, let it all out,' she soothes whilst gently rubbing my back.

I open my eyes the next morning and find that I made it into my own bedroom. 'Ouch! Bright lights!' I splutter. My mouth… urgh…what happened? Oh! I remember the night before… The drink, the kiss, the sick… Hang on – the kiss. The break-up. Danny dumped me. I start sobbing into my pillow. Danny's out of my life now. I don't even know if I'll ever see him again. He's moving to London. With someone else. It feels like he died.

'Enough crying over that dick! You'll get all puffy-eyed again.' Steph's muffled voice comes from under the duvet. I lift my head up and see the outline of Steph's body under the covers next to me. I pull back the duvet. 'Hey!' she cries. 'Put that back! It's too damn bright in here!'

'Sorry,' I say, lying back down and pulling the cover over both our heads.

'You OK, babes?' She grabs my hand and turns to face me.

'No, not really,' I manage through streaming tears.

'Look, you need a duvet day to get all this crying out of your system. We can just chill, watch chick flicks and eat junk. You can cry some more, we can eat junk some more...repeat!'

'This is why you're my best friend!' I say, pulling her in for a hug.

'Yeah, but you might wanna think about brushing your teeth, hon... Just sayin'!'

I pull back. 'Oh yeah...sick. Sorry about that! Thanks for having my hair.'

'That's what drunk friends are for!'

CHAPTER TWO

It's Monday morning and I'm sat at my desk with zero motivation. It's 11:30 and I think I've only answered one email. Lauren strolls over in her monochrome skirt suit that hugs every curve perfectly and makes me feel even worse than I already do.

'Amy, are you OK, my lovely? You seem a bit quiet today?'

I look up from my screen trying to put a smile on my face. 'I'm OK thanks. What can I do for you, Lauren?'

'You're not OK! Shall we go and grab a coffee and you can tell me all about it?'

'Coffee sounds great to be honest!' I push myself up from my desk and straighten out my skirt.

We walk into the coffee shop and Lauren orders our coffees. 'Muffin?' she asks, raising one eyebrow.

'No thanks – not got much of an appetite.' I make my way over to a table as she pays and start playing with the sugar sachets.

She sits opposite and folds her arms on top of the table. Then she leans over, knocks the sugar out of my hands and says, 'Come on then, spill!'

I instantly start crying again. I don't know what's the matter with me! It's like a sprinkler tap and I just can't turn it off. I just feel so lost.

'Hey, come on now, it can't be that bad whatever it is,' she says, handing me a packet of tissues.

The coffees are brought over, and I hide my face in a tissue until the server has left. This is so embarrassing. I really need to get control of this. 'It's Danny,' I tell Lauren. 'He's going to live in London, with some other woman. He's left me for some other woman!' And right on cue, my eyes are bursting with water again. 'I'm so sorry, Lauren, I just can't stop crying. I thought it would have stopped by now. My head physically hurts; my eyes ache. I just want to get over him already!'

She places her hand on mine and says, 'Honey, you need to let it all out. Once you've cried it all out, you'll be done. You really need something to take your mind off him. And honestly, I don't think he's worth your precious tears. You know what I think you need?'

'What?' I ask, curling my hands around my steaming latte.

'A holiday!' She beams at me whilst making jazz hands in the air.

'Like I could afford that!' I reply, sipping my latte and rolling my eyes.

'You can if you borrow my villa in the Canaries!' And out come the jazz hands again.

'Lauren, that would be AMAZING! Honestly, for free?' I gaze up with my mouth agape. Nobody ever gives you anything for free.

'Yeah, course. I'm pretty sure it's empty right now. I can speak to Daddy to make sure.'

I immediately pull my phone out of my bag and start typing a message to Steph: *Fancy a week in the Canary Islands?! xx*. I think this is exactly what I need. Some sunshine, relaxation and cocktails. My phone beeps. I open Steph's reply: *OMG babes, deffo!! Just let me know when and I'll book time off work! xxx*. I look up at Lauren. 'This means so much to me, thank you!'

'Of course,' she says with a shrug. 'It's no bother, and you've always been so nice. And you work really hard. You deserve a break. And he does *not* deserve you!'

I meet Steph in town straight after work so I can max out my store card on a new wardrobe. She links arms with me and is practically skipping me down the street.

'This is so freaking awesome, Ames! Sunshine, margaritas, hot men…in tiny trunks!' She wiggles her eyebrows up and down and gives me a mischievous grin.

The heat blasts down on me and blows my hair into my face as soon as we walk through the shop doors.

'Yeah, I think you may need a teeny-weeny makeover too, my sweet. No offence! But like, when was the last time you had a haircut? Like a proper one, in a salon?'

I brush my hair out of my face and give her a look that says, '*Really?*' But inside, I think she's right. I'm always just giving it a quick trim myself to save money. It probably could do with a proper cut. And actually, I feel quite excited about getting a fresh new look. New hair, new make-up, new clothes, new me! Just what I need. Or rather, the old me.

This is so much fun! I can't remember the last time I had a blowout like this. And I can't remember the last time I chose clothes for me and not Danny. With Steph's encouragement, I'm picking up borderline slutty clothes, and I'm so excited to try them on!

My arms are aching from the amount of clothes hanging over them. I enter the changing room and hang them all up. I put on a white and gold bikini which Steph picked out, and I'm expecting to hate it. My tummy is going to be hanging over it. I'm going to look ridiculous on a beach next to Steph. As I pull on the briefs, I realise they're high-waisted and really quite flattering. I check the label. It's a size ten. I'm amazed. Danny always said I looked better in a swimming costume. I pull the top on. It has a halterneck and a thick wrap-around band across the ribs just under the bust. I love it! If it were flimsy and delicate I think I'd feel exposed, but there's enough material to feel that I'm suitably covered up.

'Amy, come out and show me already. You must have something on by now!' Steph calls.

I peer behind the curtain to see her standing there in the skimpiest red bikini and wearing a pair of heels. With hands on hips, she has an impatient look on her face. 'Steph, you look drop-dead gorge!' I gasp. 'But you may be drawing a little attention to yourself!' I tilt my head in the direction of a man who looks old enough to be her granddad. He's standing outside the changing rooms gawping at her.

She giggles and pushes me backwards, joining me in my dressing room. 'Oh, Ames. You look stunning! I can't remember the last time I saw you show some skin! You need to own that body! Work it, girl!' As she dances around me clicking her fingers, I feel myself flush.

'I don't look as bad as I was expecting! I was surprised I could even get it on,' I say, looking at both of us in the mirror.

'Your problem, babe, is that prick has been knocking your confidence for years now.' Steph puts her arm around my waist and rests her head on my shoulder. 'I've been trying to tell you for so long, but you were so in love, and I didn't want to push it too much and lose you. You are so much more beautiful than you give yourself credit for. Oh shoot, you've got an appointment in an hour. Hurry and try the rest of this stuff on!' With that, she kisses me on the top of my head and runs out to change.

I think she's right. Without Danny putting doubts in my head, I think I'm starting to feel more confident about myself. I look at my reflection and hold my head up high, hands on hips and pout. I think I'm finding myself again.

We go over to the MAC counter where I take a seat. What is all this stuff? What does it all do? I have make-up, but this is another level!

The lady on the counter holds my chin in her hands and sways my head from side to side. 'We are gonna make you look so hot,' she says and winks at me. She is chewing gum and looks about eighteen.

I'm not sure about this, but twenty minutes, five palettes and ten brushes later, she hands me a mirror. Wow! 'How did you do that?' I ask, amazed. My eyes look wonderful, and the coverage on my skin... I can't see one blemish.

'Absolutely gorgeous!' Steph squeals as she claps jumping on the spot.

'I guess I'll take it all!' I announce, handing over my store card.

I pick up all my bags feeling elated and we start heading towards the exit. Steph then runs over to a gorgeous dress. It's all flowy and flowery and screams summer.

'Oh, Steph! It's beautiful!' I say as I feel the silk in between my fingers and reach for the price tag. 'OMG! Have you seen the price of this thing? It's not *that* nice!'

She glances at the price. 'It *is* that nice, babe! Glamour doesn't come cheap! You have to have it!'

'What? I can't! There's no way I can justify that much money on one outfit!'

She pulls a size ten off the rail and marches me towards the dressing room. 'You can. You've got me a week in a villa for free. I figure I owe you at least this much!'

'Exactly, Steph, free! I didn't pay; you don't owe me anything!'

She yanks me into the fitting room and slides the curtain across. 'Amy, you've got me a free week in the sun. I've got you the perfect outfit to get laid. Score's even. Now try the damn thing on!'

CHAPTER THREE

It's Wednesday, 3 p.m., and I'm sat in the hair salon where Steph has booked me an appointment. I'm nervous. I don't know what I want doing, and Steph can't make it because she's stuck at work. I want to just leg it. Lauren let me leave early especially, so if I don't go into work tomorrow with a new hairdo she's going to know about it! I'm flicking through magazines but can't find anything that seems 'me'. Oh no, someone's heading towards me.

'Amy?' she asks.

'Yes, that's me,' I say through gritted teeth and smiling nervously. She has shocking red hair that is very, very short. I mean, it looks great on her...she has the petite little face for it, but what if she tries to do that to me?

She sits me down in front of a mirror and ties a gown around my neck. 'What can we do for you today then, sweetheart?' she asks whilst resting her hands on the back of the chair.

'Just a trim really.' I shrug.

She raises her eyebrows. 'I'm going to be honest, Amy. I do Steph's hair, and when she booked you in she said you'd probably say that, and that I was to ignore you.'

I sit open-mouthed in disbelief, but I'm feeling more relaxed now. If she does Steph's hair, it can't be that bad. 'What do you think I should have done, then?' I ask. 'I know I haven't been to a proper hairdresser for a really long time, but I like my hair long!' I pull a sad pout.

'I'm not a butcher!' she reassures me and rubs my shoulder. 'But your hair is very long, and I think it needs a good cut. We can still keep the length, though. I promise! And we'll probably give you a decent conditioning treatment to release some of this frizz!'

'OK – do it! Before I change my mind!' I say, hiding my face underneath my hands.

'What about colour?' she asks, tilting her head.

'Colour? What's wrong with brown?' I ask, peering over my hands. Oh no, she's going to make it red, or purple, or blue!

'Nothing's wrong with brown, sweetheart. I just think some highlights could really lift it. I promise you won't regret it. A few caramels, and coppery tones, that's all! I'll go and mix your colours and fetch you a tea? Coffee?'

'Coffee, thanks.' I can't believe I'm agreeing to this.

I leave the salon feeling like a million dollars! I had a shock at first; she's cut about four inches off the length! As soon as I noticed all my hair on the floor, I thought I was going to hate it. But it's so bouncy and shiny and wavy! She's given my hair a new lease of life! I don't know why I didn't do it ages ago! Well, yes I do, because it was mega expensive...but it was a hundred per cent worth it! It's only been five days since we broke up, and I'm still sad. I still find myself crying every day when something random reminds me of him. But I'm also feeling more like *me* again. I feel myself getting stronger. My confidence is growing by the bucketload.

As I arrive home, I walk through the front door and Mum shouts, 'Whitwoo!'

'Do you like it, Mum?' I ask, showing off my new bouncy waves.

'I think it's stunning, darling! How are you holding up? Have you heard from him?'

'What, Danny? No, why would I?'

She looks at me full of sympathy. 'I just thought you pair might have worked things out by now, that's all, love.'

'There's nothing to sort out, Mum. It's over. He has someone else.'

'And good riddance!' grumbles Dad as he walks into the kitchen.

'He wasn't that bad!' replies Mum.

Dad puts his arms around my shoulders, pulls me in for a squeeze and kisses my forehead. 'No one will ever be good enough for my Amy!' Which makes me feel like I'm still ten.

I don't push him away, though. As much as I hate to admit it, it feels nice. It's just the comfort I need. Knowing I have my parents to lean on means the world to me. Although, I sometimes feel that Mum is fighting Danny's corner. I wish she would stick by me more. Sometimes it feels as though she prefers Danny to me. I'm sure she doesn't, I tell myself.

'You've got a new posh hairdo!' Dad declares.

'Yes, I got it done this afternoon. You like it?' I ask.

'Looks lovely, but you always do in my opinion, love, you know that.'

'Tea, darling?' asks Mum.

'To be honest, I'd prefer a wine,' I say as I sit at the kitchen table.

'Wine? On a Wednesday?' she asks.

'Mum, I'm having a bad week, if you haven't noticed! Tea just isn't going to cut it. I'm sorry to disappoint you...'

'Oh, it's not disappointing, darling! I've got a lovely bottle of Sauvignon Blanc in the fridge, and I thought I'd have to wait until Friday! You're giving me an excuse to open it early!'

Surprised, I turn towards the fridge and reach for the bottle of wine. I turn back to Dad. 'Are you having a glass?'

'No thanks, love. If you girls are starting on the wine, I'm going down The Bull for a quiet pint. If that's alright with you, Sue?' he asks Mum with a pleading look in his eyes. Poor Dad, he's hardly ever allowed down the pub because once he starts, he will be gone for at least four hours when he gets chatting with all his mates.

'It's fine, Jim,' Mum says with a sigh. 'It's curry and a pint night for six pounds, isn't it?'

'Yes, I believe so, love,' says Dad, looking hopeful.

'Get your dinner there, then. We both know you'll never be back in time for dinner here!' she utters, pulling two wine glasses out of the cupboard and placing them on the table.

Dad kisses us both on the cheek and runs out through the front door before Mum has a chance to change her mind.

It's starting to get dark and we're still sat in the kitchen. We finished the white wine and moved on to a bottle of red. When that ran out, we moved on to some Baileys we found in the back of the cupboard left over from Christmas. I'm sure I've consumed most of it, but we're both rather drunk, and I'm starting to regret drinking so much on a school night.

'I know you think I'm siding with Danny,' Mum begins, 'but I assure you I'm not. I wouldn't ever take anyone's side over yours. You are my precious daughter. And you mean the world to me! I just thought Danny was going to be your way out of this house.'

I look up at my mum in disbelief. 'What, you want me to get out of your house?' I ask, tears stinging the back of my eyes.

'No, no, darling! You know you're always welcome here! I would have you live here forever! But *you* can't want that! When I was your age, I was already married and living with your dad. And we'd have had a whole herd of kids if we were able. It took us so long to be blessed with you that we never had the chance to have any more kids. I know times have changed, and it's harder to get your foot on the property ladder nowadays, but I worry about you. What if it takes you as long as it took me to conceive? I just worry by the time you settle down it will be too late. You won't be able to have a family of your own.'

I see a tear running down her cheek. 'Mum!' I take her hand in mine and give it a squeeze. 'I never knew you wanted more than me. It would've been nice having a sibling growing up. I always wanted one.'

'I know you did, sweetheart. You used to ask me for a baby brother or sister all the time, and it used to break my heart that I couldn't give it to you!'

There are more tears now. I've never seen my mum this upset before. I lean over to the counter and grab the box of tissues, pushing them towards her. 'I'm sorry, Mum.'

'Don't be sorry, love! It's not your fault! I just don't want you to have the same problems as me. I thought you and Danny might move in together soon and get married and then you could start a family. And now you've got to start all over again,' she wails and pulls a tissue to her face to blow her nose.

'Mum, I don't even know if I want kids,' I start, trying to ease her worries.

'What do you mean you don't want kids!' she yells.

I take a deep breath. 'I'm not saying I don't want them for sure... I just don't have any real desires for children yet. I'm not saying I won't want any in the future. But yeah, it'd be nice to be out from under your roof. I thought I'd be moving in with Danny too. It was such a shock when he announced he was leaving me. I never expected it. But I'm starting to think it might be a good thing.'

'I have to say, dear, looking at you, it does seem to be doing wonders for your image!' says Mum. 'I just worry you're not eating very much; you need to keep your strength up, darling!'

I take another deep breath and roll my eyes. 'I'm not starving myself, Mum. I'm eating enough – just probably not eating loads any more. That's what happens when you get comfortable, isn't it? You overeat!'

'I don't think you could ever overeat, love, you're such a skinny minny! I wish I had your metabolism,' she says, downing the last of her Baileys.

'Danny didn't make me feel like I was all that skinny, to be honest.' I reach for my drink. I swill the dregs of the silky Baileys around the bottom of my glass before sliding it down my throat until it's all gone. 'I'm starting to think Danny wasn't very good for my confidence at all. I just don't know why I never noticed before.'

'Aw, my lovey. You're better off rid of him if he didn't make you feel good! You deserve better than that. At least you have your holiday with Steph to look forward to. That's exciting!'

A big smile spreads across my face. 'It really is exciting! The last time I went away was with Danny to Majorca. And that was what…about two and a half years ago! I remember having an OK time, but the more I think about it, the more I realise I just went along with whatever Danny wanted to do. Don't get me wrong, it was still nice, but we sat in the same bar watching the footy most nights because it was the World Cup. And I don't mind that… Well, I guess I do mind that. I'd rather have just watched the England match and gone to other bars and restaurants every other night. I mean, we had meals in a basket for God's sake, in front of a projector screen, with a load of rowdy Englishmen. I might as well have spent the week in The Bull! The days were OK, I suppose. We went on a couple of excursions and relaxed around the pool, but I think my holiday with Steph is going to be so much more *fun*!'

'Good for you, darling!' she says, getting up from the table. 'Your dad will probably be back soon; I'd better get the kitchen cleaned up. But I'm so glad you're happy. At least, you seem to be getting a little happier?'

I stand up and take our glasses over to the sink. 'Do you know what, Mum, I think I am… I think I am.'

CHAPTER FOUR

It's lunchtime on Thursday and I'm scoffing a Tesco chicken and bacon sandwich at my desk whilst searching for cheap flights to Lanzarote. Lauren sneaks up behind me. 'Working hard, eh?' she says, jabbing me in the sides and making me yelp in surprise.

'Oh, Lauren, jeez! You scared the life out of me!' I realise that three-quarters of the office are looking in my direction wondering what the commotion is. How embarrassing! There are a few people I get on with in the office, but most of them are so much older than me, and they all think they're so much more important than me, so I just can't be bothered to speak to them any more than the required co-worker politeness.

'Sorry, hon! Didn't mean to frighten you!' She pulls up a chair. 'Well, your hair looks fabulous, but I have to say, you don't look great… Are you feeling OK?'

I lick the mayo off my lips and wipe the crumbs away with my sleeve. 'Sorry, Lauren, I was starving – skipped breakfast coz I got up late. I might've had one too many drinks for a school night!'

She tuts as she tosses her shiny coppery hair over her shoulder. 'On a school night, eh? Out on the town, was we? Showcasing your new *do*? I *love* it, by the way… Looks totally gorge – really suits you!'

'Aw, thanks,' I say, feeling myself blush. 'I really love it, too! But I wasn't out. I was just at home with my mum. We had a bit of a heart to heart actually; it was quite nice.'

'Aww, that's so sweet! A bit of mummy-daughter time. Just what you need right now. So, you're checking out the flights, I see!' She nods her head towards my computer screen.

'Yeah, well I've been checking every day hoping they will come down, but they just seem to be getting more expensive!'

'Here—' she budges me out of the way '—allow me.' After ten

minutes of changing departure dates and flicking between departure airports, she tilts the screen towards me. 'This one, this is your cheapest option, leaving Saturday evening. And it works out cheaper for some reason if you do ten days. How's that for you?'

'That's amazing! Thank you, Lauren! I'll check with Steph now and book it!'

She pushes herself up from my desk. 'You are going to have the *best* time – trust me! We've been going there for many years. It's such a beautiful place and the locals are all so welcoming. I guarantee you'll see someone so attractive you'll be thinking... *Danny who?*' She shrugs raising her eyebrows and letting out a little giggle.

I laugh and reach for my phone to call Steph. 'I'm really not after anyone else. Just having some time in the sun with my best friend will be great!'

'Yeah, yeah. We'll see!' she calls as she struts back to her office.

I call Steph. She agrees to the flight dates and times straight away and transfers the money into my account. This is it, then. I book the flights and spend the rest of the afternoon ordering last-minute items from Boots: sun cream, miniature toiletries, travel adapters. I feel bad that I haven't done a stitch of work today in my hungover state.

Just as I'm about to leave work, I get a text from Danny. My heart starts pounding in my chest. What can he want? What if he wants to get back together when I've just booked this holiday? Part of me longs for the familiar feeling of his arm around my waist, his mouth against mine. 'Don't be an idiot,' I whisper to myself. I know it'd be so much easier to slip back into my old routine of life with Danny. But really, being out of the relationship has given me perspective. I know I can be better without him now. I can get back to the old Amy. But why do I feel so alone, and unwanted.

I close my eyes and take a deep breath before opening the message: *Hi Amy, hope u r ok? Back at flat tomorrow, do you want to come and get your things? Be there between 10am & 1pm x.*

Is that all? I'm a little disappointed it's not a grovelling apology asking me to come back. Not that I would go back – but obviously it would feel pretty damn good if he wanted me back and things had gone wrong with his London lover. I don't even know what I've left at his flat. It can't be anything important. A spare toothbrush, maybe a couple of items of clothing. Then I remember. My nan's bracelet! Dammit! I text Steph, *Can you meet me at The Bull in 20? Need to talk! xx.* Her reply is instant: *Course babe, be 20-30 mins, get me a pint in xx.*

I walk into the pub and make my way to the bar. Why do I feel like everyone is looking at me? The penny drops. Oh yeah, last time I was in here there was a bit of a scene. I keep my head down, take a seat at the bar and pull my phone out of my bag whilst waiting to be served. I hate being sat in a pub on my own. I wonder what it would have been like years ago when we didn't have a mobile phone to entertain us while waiting for our friends.

Looking up, I notice a couple of my dad's mates across the bar. They give me a wave, and I smile and wave back. It's such an old man's pub. It's dark and dingy and smells of stale ale, probably because the drip trays are full to the brim, I notice. I can't wait to be sat on a beach drinking a cocktail. Just sitting in this pub makes me feel depressed.

'What can I get ya, darl?' the landlady asks, looking at me, hands resting on the beer pumps.

'Er, a pint of lager and half a cider, please.' I can't face any more wine after last night. Just as I'm handing over the money, Steph strolls over and perches on the stool next to me.

'Heyyyy!' she says, pulling me in for a hug and kissing me on the cheek. 'We're going on holiday on Saturday! Woop! Woop!' and she's doing a little jig in her seat.

'Yeah! Can't wait!' I reply, and I mean it. The thought of the holiday instantly lifts my mood.

'Cheers!' She picks up her pint and clinks it against my glass. 'So, what do we need to talk about? Who is taking hair straighteners? Curlers? Are we sharing shoes?'

'Well, yeah *all* of that! But also, I've had a text from Danny. He wants me to collect my stuff from his place. I thought whatever it was I could just leave, but then I remembered the bracelet my nan left me. It's there. At his stupid flat. In his stupid bedside drawers. I can't leave that there! I need to get it back!' I wail.

She puts her arm around me and makes a shushing sound. 'Hey now, don't be upset. It's fine. You can get it back, babe; he's offering it you back!'

'But that means I have to see him again! I'm not sure I can face him.' I take a long swig of my drink.

'I can come with you, if you want?' She is my soldier. Love her!

'Ah, I would love that, but I have to go at lunchtime tomorrow. He says he's only there until one.'

'Oh yeah, sorry, babe. There's no way I can get out of work. I'll be working until about eight every night this week, trying to tie up all my loose ends before we go away. But you can do it, hon! Be strong! Go there, get your stuff and get out! And before you know it, we'll be sat on an aeroplane heading for sunshine, sipping Prosecco!'

Even though I'm still dreading seeing Danny tomorrow, I can't help but feel buzzed about my holiday with Stephanie. Just being around her lifts my soul and I feel as though I could conquer the world.

We spend the next three hours in the pub discussing who is taking what. Detailing every outfit down to the costume jewellery, shoes and bags to match so that neither of us are taking any unnecessary weight in our luggage. We're flying on a budget airline, and they're extremely tight on the baggage allowance. Steph's clothes will probably be a little snug on me, but I think they'll fit. And we're both a size five shoe. Although, I'm a bit apprehensive about wearing Steph's shoes. All of hers are about two inches taller than mine! I'll probably be walking like Bambi on ice! Talking about the holiday completely takes my mind off having to see Danny.

The next morning at work, Lauren comes bounding straight over to my desk. 'Hiya! Here's the address to the villa along with the keys. I've also written you a list of restaurant recommendations, there's a taxi number and directions to the local shop.'

'Wow, thanks, Lauren! That's so nice of you. I still can't believe you're letting me stay there for nothing! You've been so nice. I can't thank you enough!'

'That's quite alright, lovely!' She leans over with her arms out for a hug. I realise a bit late that she's trying to hug me and meet her twenty per cent of the way to her eighty. I just wasn't expecting it. She is the boss after all – it just feels a little awkward.

'I have a little something here for you.' I bend down and pick up a bottle bag and card from under my desk and hand them over to her. 'It's not much, but I felt like I needed to get you a little something, to show my appreciation!'

'Ah, that's so sweet! Thanks. You really didn't have to get me anything! But thank you, it means a lot.'

'It's nothing much really; don't get your hopes up!' I think she's going to look in the bag and be really disappointed when she discovers it's an eight-pound bottle of red wine. It should have been ten, though; it was on offer in Tesco's. I popped in to get it on my way into the office. I'd never usually spend over six on a bottle personally, so I thought it must be a nice one. I imagine she's only used to vintage expensive wine. I doubt she'll even drink it. She'll probably just regift it to someone else. Still, the thought was there. The way I see it, she knows what she pays me; therefore, she knows what I can afford.

She opens the thank-you card and smiles reading it. She pulls the bottle out of the bag. 'Shiraz! I love Shiraz!' She pulls me in for another hug. 'Thank you. I know we only see each other at work and I'm your boss, but I'd like to think that we're friends too. You're the only person near my age in this place let's face it!

And I really enjoy our chats over coffee. I wouldn't be offering you our family villa if I didn't consider you a friend. So, keep me posted! I want daily updates on any new man action! Got it?'

'Absolutely!' I reply. 'Although, I'm sure if there's any man action, it will all be to do with Steph, but I will keep you fully informed! And I think of you as a friend, too, of course. Thanks again, Lauren.'

'No worries!' she says and walks back to her office. 'Oh, don't forget to sort out those figures for me before you go today though, please! And don't forget to set your Out of Office on your mailbox. Direct all your emails to Derek.'

Derek looks up from his desk with a 'Why me?' expression, and I try to stifle a snort. The poor man is hanging on for retirement and tries to get away with doing as little as he possibly can. About time he did some actual work; he's probably being paid triple my salary, if not more.

I pull up outside Danny's flat at lunchtime. I'm in front of a removals van, and I can see his VW Golf parked on the other side of the road. This must be his removal van. He must be leaving already. Is this going to be the last time I ever see him? I'm so upset and angry, and there's a horrible feeling in my stomach. I don't want to see him, I'm not ready to see him, yet the thought of never seeing him ever again fills me with dread.

The removal van pulls around me and drives off down the road. Shit. I check the time. It's 12:30. Well, his car is still here, so he must be here. I hope he's got my nan's bloody bracelet.

With the sudden worry that my nan's bracelet might still be sat in his bedside drawers which look like they're already on the way to London, I jump out of the car and walk over to the flat. I still have keys, I realise, when I automatically lift my car keys as I reach the entrance to the flats. I should have just come over last night to get it and avoided seeing him altogether. Maybe deep down I wanted to see him again.

I use the fob to enter the foyer and walk up the flight of stairs. As I'm about to put my key in the lock, I stop myself. I knock on the door. I don't have the right to let myself in any more.

'Alright, Ames?' he says, stepping back to let me in. He's wearing dark blue jeans and a crisp white T-shirt. His hair is all ruffled and sexy, and he has a day's worth of stubble that somehow makes him look more irresistible. Just seeing him makes my stomach clench. I want nothing more than to put my arms around him and feel his body against mine.

I enter the flat and as I walk past him, I breathe in the scent of his aftershave, which just makes me want him more. I shouldn't have come here. I can't do this. I look around the flat. At least it's empty now. There are fewer memories. Less chance of me suddenly bursting into tears and making a fool of myself.

He hands me a bag. 'Here's your things, Ames. I'm so sorry about everything.'

I take the bag and peer inside. A few items of clothing, toothbrush, deodorant, perfume. I pull out a sandwich bag and see that it contains my nan's bracelet. 'Thanks,' I say, relieved. 'I was so worried you'd sent my nan's bracelet to London.'

'Come on, Ames, I wouldn't do that. I know how much that bracelet means to you. You look nice... You changed your hair?'

'Um...yeah, thanks.' We stand in silence looking at each other. God, he looks hot. (I obviously also made the effort to look good this morning to remind him what he's missing. What self-respecting ex-girlfriend wouldn't?) 'I'd best get going, then; let you get on with your new life,' I say as I start to walk towards the door.

But he steps forward and steers me sideways until my back is against the cold wall. He has one arm stretched out leaning on the wall, his hand by the side of my face, and the other is holding my hip. He bends his head down to mine and kisses me.

It feels so natural, kissing Danny, so familiar. I feel his large, soft hand start to slide underneath my shirt, and his other hand slides down to touch my face and pull me closer, deeper into the kiss. It takes me a moment to remember, to realise the situation.

As much as I don't want to, I try to push him away. 'Danny, we can't do this. We're not together any more. You have someone else.'

'I know,' he says, breathing hard against my cheek. He presses his body against mine, and I can feel that he wants me. As he starts kissing my neck, I feel all the fight leave my body. I want him. And he wants me. All that matters in this moment is that we want each other. I drop the bag to the floor and pull him against me, my desire taking over.

Afterwards feels so awkward. What a moment ago felt so natural and right, now feels so weird and wrong. He hasn't even said anything. He just zipped up his jeans and walked away. Why did I just let that happen? I'm so angry with myself.

I go to the bathroom to try and freshen myself up. I can feel tears rolling down my cheeks, which I wipe away with the back of my hand. I can't let him see me like this. 'Don't let him get the better of you!' I whisper to myself.

He knocks on the door. 'Amy, I need to go.'

'Coming,' I reply in a broken voice. I flush the loo, wash my hands and splash my face with a little cold water. I have to use loo roll to dry my hands and dab my face because there's nothing left in the bathroom, not one towel.

As I walk out, he's waiting by the front door. After picking up my bag of belongings, I take his keys off my key ring and hand them to him.

'Oh, cheers,' he says whilst holding open the door for me to walk through.

'Bye then?' I say, walking out.

'Yeah, see ya,' he says.

I get back into my car and throw the bag onto the passenger seat. *See ya! Bloody see ya!* I'm seething. A four-year relationship, and *that's* how he says goodbye? And what was that? What just happened in there? What did I let him do to me? I'm so angry with myself!

I see him emerge from the flats and run across the road to his car. He doesn't even acknowledge me. I feel like such a bloody fool. 'Bugger off to London then, you bastard!' I mutter as I start up my car and head back to the office.

CHAPTER FIVE

It's Saturday. I spent all night in my room crying, feeling used and horrible after my encounter with Danny. I haven't even told Steph yet. I can't bring myself to tell her; I feel so ashamed. I've spent the day packing and I'm just printing off our boarding passes. The taxi should be here in an hour, and I'll pick up Steph en route. I'm so glad I've been busy all day; it's kept my mind occupied instead of thinking back to yesterday's sordidness.

I'm crossing everything off my 'to pack' list when Mum walks in. 'I see you managed to get the printer to work then, love. Well done. I can't ever get the blooming thing to work.'

'Yes, it worked fine,' I say, lifting off the boarding passes. Grinning, I wiggle them in front of her face before placing them in my handbag.

'Here, me and your dad want you to take this.' She hands me a card.

I read the front. 'Travel money card?' I ask.

'Yes, we've loaded it with euros for you!'

'What? Why?' I ask stunned, and also wondering idly how much 'loaded' means.

She sits down next to me and places a hand on my knee. 'Well, me and your dad have a bit of money put away, and we know you don't have much. We don't want you running out of money, do we now? And we don't want you to miss out on doing things because you can't afford it.'

I put my arms around her and give her a big squeeze. 'Thanks so much, Mum. That's amazing! I don't know what to say!'

She squeezes me back. 'That's alright, darling. Now, don't go bringing us back any souvenir tat will you! We don't need anything. We just want you to have a fantastic time and come back our happy little girl again.'

I laugh. 'No tat – I promise! Thanks, Mum!'

As the taxi pulls up outside Steph's, I see her yanking her case over the doorstep. She looks so glamorous. Here's me in leggings, T-shirt, denim jacket and my Converse, opting for comfort over style for the flight. She's wearing a red and white maxi dress, a white blazer with three-quarter length sleeves and a big floppy white sun hat with a black band around it.

She walks to the back of the car, hands her suitcase to the taxi driver and then clambers in, slinging her large beach bag down by her feet. 'Ready?' she squeals with excitement.

'*Soooo* ready!' I reply. 'You look amazing! I didn't realise we were making an effort for the plane,' I say, gesturing to my attire.

'Ah, don't be daft. You look great! I just had to wear some stuff because room in my case was really tight! Check this!' She lifts her wrist and jangles lots of bangles. 'Weigh a ton these things, so thought I'd just wear 'em!'

'That's actually quite genius. I'm guessing that's also why you're wearing a sun hat?'

'You got it! I mean, I know I look ridiculous now, but I'll fit right in as soon as we're in the airport!'

Once we're at the airport and our bags have been checked in and we're past the security clearance, we head for the duty-free shopping. We walk through the perfume section. I could do with a new scent. I've been wearing the same perfume for years now because it's what Danny liked. Mum and Dad have been kind enough to give me some spending money. No harm in me splashing out a little and treating myself. After I've sniffed about six different perfumes, they're all starting to smell the same and my head is feeling a little dizzy.

'Ames!' Steph calls. 'You have to smell this one – it's divine!'

As I walk over, she shoves her wrist into my face. 'Mmm, yeah...that smells gorgeous!' I look at the price. 'Eighty-five quid! I thought these were supposed to be cheaper in the airport!'

Steph rolls her eyes at me. 'Amy, this is some strong stuff. You don't have to coat yourself in it like the cheap ones! A couple of sprays is all you'll need, babe. It'll last longer, so it's well worth parting with your hard-earned cash; plus, you'll smell irresistible. You'll have hordes of men following you down the beach like that Lynx advert!'

'Well, *that's* got to be worth eighty-five pounds now, hasn't it!' I giggle as I pick up the eighty-millilitre bottle and head to the counter. As I pull out my purse to pay, I notice a twenty-pound note with a bright pink Post-it note stuck to it. I hand my card and boarding pass to the cashier and pull out the note. It says, *For at the airport! Have fun darling. Mum & Dad xxx.* Ah, bless them, they are so sweet. I take back my card and boarding pass, loading them into my bag, but I fold the money in my hand.

'Right, enough shopping, hon, it's time for a drink! I can see a fizz bar over there!' Steph says as she links her arm through mine and practically marches me to the bar. I'm almost running to keep up with her.

'Thirsty, are we?' I ask in between laughing.

'You know it, babe!' She sits me down at a table and plonks her bag on the floor.

As she's about to go over to the bar, I shout, 'Oh, here!' and hand her the money with the note still attached. 'I'll get this one.' She starts to protest. 'No, open it,' I say.

She opens it up and reads the note. 'Aww! Your mum and dad. Legends! First one's on Sue and Jim, then!' She comes back with two glasses of Prosecco and sits down opposite me. Lifting her glass, she says, 'Cheers! Here's to an awesome holiday!' We clink glasses.

'Cheers! So, there's no time difference in Lanzarote, and the flight is four hours, so we should land about nine-ish,' I muse.

'Nine...hmmm... So you wanna go out tonight? Or chill when we get there and go explore in the morning?'

'Yeah, probably just chill tonight, if that's OK?' I'm feeling rather tired after crying all night and running around packing all day. I'm not sure I could face having to get ready and go out after a four-hour flight. The Prosecco is delicious and crisp and goes down far too quickly.

'Another?' she asks before downing the rest of her glass.

'Yes please!'

The barman then appears with another two glasses.

'Oh, we didn't order yet, did we?' I ask.

'I've told him to keep them coming – paid for us to have four each,' she says, winking at me. 'Thank you, Steve, you're a good 'un!' she adds with a flirty smile.

His cheeks flush, and he puts the glasses in front of us and takes away the empties.

'Thanks…Steve,' I say. I then look at Steph.

'What?' she asks all innocently.

'He looks about fifteen! Stephanie Wood! You'd eat that poor boy alive!'

She giggles. 'It's only a bit of harmless flirting so he keeps bringing the drinks over, and he must be at least eighteen to serve alcohol, right? Besides, he's quite cute!'

'Well, yeah, he is quite cute.' I find myself ogling his boyish good looks and shy smile whilst biting my bottom lip.

'Stop staring, then! He's looking right at you!' Steph gently kicks me under the table and pulls me out of my daydream. 'Bad girl!' she says, mockingly wagging her finger at me and then throwing her head back laughing.

'Sorry!' I say, turning back to her and drinking the last of my drink, again. Wow, these are going down fast. Straight away he's on his way over with two more. I have to turn so I'm looking in the opposite direction. I use my hand to shield my face so he can't see me giggling like a schoolgirl. As he leaves the table with the two empty glasses, Steph and I look at each other and burst into fits of laughter. 'Sorry, I don't know what's the matter with me!' I giggle.

'I do!' she declares. 'You're in need of some action!'

'Well, you're right there. It doesn't help that I was left unsatisfied yesterday.' Oh shit. That just slipped out.

'What! With who? Oh, not Danny? Amyyyy!'

I cover my face with my hands. 'Yeah, kind of just happened. I tried to stop it. Well, I didn't try very hard to be honest. I kind of wanted it to happen. When I could see him, smell him, feel him... I wanted him. But then it was all over so quick. He just got what he wanted, then walked away and left me there, wanting, and feeling used. I'm so angry with myself for letting it happen! And then he didn't even speak to me afterwards. I felt so humiliated!'

'Aw, babe!' says Steph, reaching for my hand. 'I can't believe he did that to you! He's such a scumbag! I hope he's fecked off to London now so he'll leave you the hell alone!'

'Yeah, he's gone... Do you know what his goodbye was after that? See ya... That's all he said... *See ya!*' I shake my head, still not able to believe that's all he had to say to me.

'That arse!' she says whilst gesturing to the barman. 'Quick, wipe that tear off your cheek before the cutie comes back! I can't believe you actually had sex with him again...but the worst thing is I can't believe he didn't even make it count. He's just plain rude! Don't you worry – we'll get you laid soon, hon, with someone ten times hotter than Danny!' She sticks her tongue between her teeth.

I pull myself together just in time for the next drink to be brought over. I can't stop smiling at him as he places the drinks in front of us and takes the empties. God, I'm drunk. I should not be flirting with a young boy, but I can't help but feel joyful when he looks at me and smiles back.

As we board the plane, it looks like we're the stragglers – the plane is rammed. We really should have checked how far away the gate was before we started drinking! And we had to dash to the loo for an emergency wee first. There was no way I was getting on a plane and waiting until we took off; I think would have wet myself.

We find our seats. There's already a man sat in the window seat. I draw the short straw and have to sit in the middle while Steph is trying to shove her bag into the overhead storage compartment. As soon as I'm sat down, she gives in, declaring there's not enough room and puts it underneath the seat in front of her. Well played, Steph, well played. I must remember to pull a similar stunt on the way back.

After glancing to the side, I smile at the guy next to me. Hmm, not bad looking. I mean, he's a bit old for me, but he has that older sophisticated gentleman thing going on. Why do men who are just starting to turn grey look so good? One strand of grey on a woman's head and we look like we've let ourselves go.

I turn to Steph and whisper in her ear, 'Eh up, he's not bad,' and nod towards my new travel buddy.

She leans into her bag pretending to get something so she can check him out. She sits straight back up. 'Are you serious, Ames? He's like about fifty! We really need to get you laid!'

The plane starts taxiing for take-off. 'Woo, this is it, Steph, we're on our way!' I can't remember the last time I was this excited. I feel like a kid at Christmas. The drinking of bubbles at record speed has probably taken my excitement level up a notch to be fair, and my judgement of a nice-looking middle-aged man.

Steph looks as excited and giddy as me. She hands over a headphone and pops the other into her ear. 'I made us a holiday playlist! All our fave tunes. This is really going to get us in the mood!'

I sit back, listen and close my eyes as the plane roars down the runway and into the air. It still amazes me how these things ever lift off the ground.

CHAPTER SIX

I wake up to being jerked around in my seat. It takes me a second to remember I'm on an aeroplane, and I realise that we're landing. I feel dribble on my chin and wipe it with my sleeve. *Ew.* I can't believe I slept for the whole journey.

'Back in the land of the living, are we?' asks Steph, handing me a bottle of water.

'OMG...thanks! You don't understand how dry my mouth is right now!' I take the bottle from her and guzzle down half of it. 'I didn't snore, did I?'

'Only cute baby snores. Nothing to worry about, babe.'

'I'm so sorry I left you on your own for the whole flight. I feel terrible! Did you have a sleep?'

'Don't worry about it, hon!' She leans down and pulls her bag from underneath the seat in front. 'I had a book all ready to go on my Kindle. I've been in my own little fantasy world for the last four hours with a dream guy called José! I've probably finally reached your level of friskiness!' she says, raising her eyebrows. Steph leans forward, looks past me and then sits back up again. 'Yep, that old dude is looking not bad at all now!'

I burst into laughter. 'Well, it's either the book making me rampant or the two Proseccos I had mid-flight impairing my judgement!' We both burst out laughing, and the guy next to us looks over with a miserable face. We stop laughing for a second to look at each other. 'Nah!' we both say before erupting into another fit of laughter.

We finally retrieve our bags from the carousel and make our way outside. I've already called a taxi using the number Lauren gave me. As soon as we step through the automatic doors, the stifling temperature hits us.

'I love that feeling of heat when you step off an aeroplane!' says Steph, opening her arms wide and tilting her head to the sky with her eyes closed. 'Far away from the damp and cold miserable weather of Damsbury!'

'Damn right!' I agree. 'Ooh, I think that taxi over there might be for us! I'll go and investigate!' I leave Steph with the cases and jog over to speak to the driver.

He's out of the taxi already and shouts, 'Amy?' in my direction.

'Yes! I'm Amy!' I declare with excitement. I turn back to Steph and give her the thumbs up. She starts walking over pulling both of our cases behind her. I show him my piece of paper from Lauren with the villa's address to confirm the destination.

He nods and takes the bags from Steph. 'Please,' he says, gesturing for us to get in.

We climb into the car, and I have a sudden panic attack. 'Shit, I didn't get any euros at the airport! I've got nothing to pay for the taxi!'

'Chill your beans!' Steph says. 'Lucky for you, I'm more organised!' She opens her purse and shows me a wad of notes.

'Oh! You're the best!' I sit back and buckle up as the driver gets in. People abroad always drive crazier than the UK. Fact. There's no way I'd leave my belt undone.

We stare out at the scenery in silence for the twenty-minute journey and trying to suss out the area. It's dark though, so it's hard to appreciate the beauty of the island. It's more the bright lights of supermarkets, bars and restaurants. Out of Steph's window, I keep glimpsing the sea. I would love to live near the sea.

The taxi takes a turn away from the main drag, but it's not long before we're making our way up a steep driveway. The driver stops in front of the villa, pulls on his handbrake and gets out.

Steph and I look at each other with mouths open wide. 'No freakin' way!' she shouts. The villa is huge! I faff around in my handbag for the keys whilst Steph pays the driver. 'You sure this is the right one, Ames?' she asks, wheeling our bags over to the massive wooden front door. 'Only, there's a couple of lights on already?'

'Probably just security lights, on a timer or something?' As I jiggle the key in the door, it opens. 'See!' I say with delight and start fumbling for the hallway light switch on the wall. As the hall illuminates and we wheel our bags inside, we stare around at the vast space in awe. 'Wow! Steph, is this place amazing or what?'

'You did good, babe! You. Did. Good!'

We close the solid front door, which echoes around the large empty space, bouncing off the marble floors. There's a staircase straight ahead with big, chunky, spacious steps. Not too narrow, so we should be able to drag our cases up those fine.

I poke my head into the doorway on the right. The light is already on in here. Quite a spacious lounge area, typical holiday villa style, but decorated with modern taste, no usual holiday terracotta. The walls are cream and there a couple of large grey sofas, ornaments, and duck-egg blue cushions and throws, as well as a large square glass coffee table with polished silver legs. It looks immaculate.

The door opposite leads to the kitchen, and the light is already on in here, too. Nothing seems out of place. I notice there's a vase of fresh flowers on the marble-top island, a vibrant colourful display and they're so fragrant and sweet.

Steph opens up the huge American-style fridge-freezer. 'Erm...this is a bit strange, Ames?' She pulls the door wide.

I can see there's water, fresh milk, juice, eggs, cheese and ham, along with six bottles of wine. Upon closer inspection by Steph, there are two white, two rosé and two sparkling. I open the cupboards and find fresh bread, various tins and condiments. There's a wine rack full to the brim, mainly bottles of red, with a few bottles of white, even champagne.

'Don't you think it's weird that there's food here?' Steph asks, pulling all the bottles out of the wine rack and inspecting each label before discarding them on the side.

'Well, it is their family villa,' I reply, putting each bottle back in its rightful place within the rack.

'But fresh food? OMG, look, there's a bowl of fruit!' She points to a dining table behind me that I hadn't even noticed.

'I guess Lauren must have got someone to stock up the place for us?' I shrug. 'She knows all the locals.'

'In that case, find us two glasses!' She reopens the fridge and pulls out a bottle of wine. 'Rosé?' she asks. 'Or would you rather stick with the bubbles?'

'Rosé sounds good to me!' I find two glasses and rinse them under the tap, although to be honest they don't have a speck of dust on them. This place is so clean. You'd expect a holiday home to have a bit of dust lying around. There are patio doors leading to the swimming pool off the kitchen. We find the key and take ourselves outside, settling down on the huge rattan furniture. 'This is the life! Cheers!' I say to Steph, clinking my glass to hers.

'Cheers, babe! This place is absolutely freakin' amazing! We haven't even been upstairs yet!'

'I know – it's beautiful! I can't believe she's letting us stay here for free!' The cold rosé tastes delicious – a nice change from the fizz earlier. Rosé always seems more like a holiday drink to me for some reason. I hardly ever drink rosé at home. I wonder if it's actually better abroad, or if it just tastes nicer because you're in a hot country. Probably the latter; all alcohol tastes better on holiday.

I look down at the pool. 'I have to dip my feet in! Come on!' I walk down the four steps, kick off my Converse and try to pull off each trainer sock whilst still holding my wine glass and keeping my balance. It's a good job I've sobered up a bit; otherwise I'd have fallen on my arse by now!

I sit down and dangle my feet over the edge. The water feels too cold at first, but it doesn't take long for my body to adjust. Cooling my feet cools down my whole body. I feel less sweaty and sticky.

Where's Steph gone? I thought she was following me. I crane my neck to try and see over the steps and past the patio furniture when I spot her strolling back over. She's removed her long dress completely. She's walking towards me in her underwear like some kind of Victoria Secrets model, with her long blonde hair gathered over one shoulder. She's holding the bottle of rosé in one hand and a large bag of crisps in another.

'What happened to the dress?' I ask as she crouches down next me, plonking the wine bottle down with a thud.

She kicks off her shoes and squeals as she plunges her feet straight into the pool. 'Fuck me that's cold!' she screams as she takes a sharp intake of breath.

'You'll get used to it in a minute,' I assure her.

'I didn't wanna get settled without snacks and more wine.' She opens the crisp packet and waves it in front of my face.

They smell good. I take a handful and shove a couple, very unladylike, into my mouth. Mmm...paprika flavour. Proper holiday crisps. I didn't realise how hungry I was until now. When was the last time I ate? 'That doesn't explain how you lost your dress!' I say, grabbing another handful of crisps.

'Oh, well I might have to wear that again, so I didn't want to ruin it. Plus, I'm melting! Well, I was before I put my feet into this freezing cold water. I'm feeling much cooler now. Top up?' She tips the bottle towards me.

'Of course!' I tilt my glass to accept a refill.

'Ooh, I know what we need! Music!' Steph stands up and shakes the drips of water from her legs before jogging up the steps.

I feel so relaxed. All the stiffness I felt in my muscles seems to have vanished already. I swish my feet in the water and lie back resting on my elbows so I can still drink my wine. To think, a few hours ago I was in cold, grey, gloomy England.

Suddenly, Usher is blasting from the doorway and I look up to see Steph walking back out with her Bluetooth speaker. She places it on the patio table and when she next emerges from the villa, she's waving a bottle of fizz in front of her.

She shimmies down the steps singing along to the music. 'Watch out!' she sings, pointing at me and bouncing her hips. She waves her hands for me to get up and join her.

Why not? I love this tune, and I am feeling a little tipsy again already! I'm up on my feet and we both merrily sing the lyrics pointing at each other. 'So I got up and followed her to the floor. She said, baby let's go!' and with that, we're dancing to the chorus, grinding our way around the pool whilst knocking back our wine. Before I know it, my glass is full again.

About twenty minutes must have gone by. We've been getting down to Beyoncé, Justin Timberlake and TLC. Dancing to all these R 'n' B classics with my bestie just never gets old. When we are drunk dancing together, it feels like we are invincible.

'I'm sorry, Steph, I'm gonna have to stop for a break. I'm just too hot!' I pull a hair bobble off my wrist and tie my hair in a bun on top of my head. The island breeze is instantly cooling the back of my neck.

'Yeah, I'm hot too... Hey! I've got an idea! Let's just dance in the pool!' She pulls my T-shirt off me before I have time to object, puts the unopened bottle of sparkling wine between her legs and uses my T-shirt to prise the cork out of the bottle. When it opens with a loud pop, she throws my T-shirt on the floor and stares at me. 'Leggings!' When a couple of seconds pass without anything happening, she shouts, 'Off! Get them off!'

'I dunno...' I start, I feel a bit exposed in my bra.

'Come on, we've got this place to ourselves! It's not like anyone's gonna see! Besides, it's just like being in a bikini!' I admit defeat and take them off. She takes the wine glass out of my hand and places it down on the floor. 'Probably not a wise idea to take glasses with us in our state! Let's just take this.' She waves the bottle above her head before taking my hand and leading me into the water.

'Cold, cold, cold, cold!' I scream, and we're laughing like a pair of hyenas. We're in up to our waists, still dancing and singing our hearts out, passing the bottle between each other and taking swigs. At one point, I lean my head too far back and the bubbles run straight up my nose. I'm a coughing, spluttering mess, but I don't care. I'm having the best time!

It takes me a few seconds to realise that the music has stopped. I look at Steph. She's just a head above the water now.

She's braver than me! As I follow her line of vision towards the villa, I instinctively scream and throw my arms around my chest still holding the bottle. There's a man standing on the patio!

'Quite the party you ladies have going on here!' he says, walking towards us.

Shit! Who the hell is this guy? What if he's a murderer? I've had way too much to drink to outrun or outsmart a psycho killer. I'm a goner. It's a cert.

'Who the fuck are you?' shouts Steph. 'Get out of our villa! You're not allowed in here!' She's got balls – I'll give her that! She'll kick him in the nuts and manage to escape. And it'll just be me left for him to cut into tiny little pieces.

'It is most definitely not *your* villa,' he says, still closing in on us.

'Well, no, it's not ours, but we're staying here!' she yells back at him.

'Oh! On whose authority might that be, then?' he asks.

I realise he hasn't yelled back once at all the abuse Steph is throwing at him. He's so calm and composed. Fuck. He a must a bloody psycho killer.

'Her boss from work! Laura!' she yells to him.

'Lauren,' I correct her.

'Bloody Lauren, then, whatever! Fact is, you shouldn't be in here, mate! So do one and let us get back to our evening!' She's so bloody brave. My hero.

'Oh! You work for us?' he asks, reaching the end of the pool and bending down to look at me eye level.

'Us?' I ask.

'Yeah. You work for Lauren?'

'Yeah.'

'Well, I do apologise. She never told me that she had invited guests. Alex,' he says, holding out his hand as an invite for me to shake it. 'I'm Lauren's brother.'

'Oh...Amy, Amy Dixon.' I take his hand in the one that isn't holding the bottle of wine. 'Shit, sorry,' I mutter, retracting my hand quickly when I realise I've left a boob exposed, albeit beneath a bra. 'And that's Steph,' I add, pointing to the bobbing head. 'Stephanie Wood, in case you need to check with Lauren.' There's not much light out here. We never got around to figuring the lighting out. We never even ventured upstairs for God's sake! The kitchen lights are on. There are some pool lights and a couple of lampposts illuminating the pool area. I think I'm thankful for that; I can hide myself in the dim light. But I'm intrigued to know what he looks like. I wish I could make him out better.

'So, are you just gonna perv on us or d'ya think you might fetch us a towel?' Steph shouts.

'Oh, I'm sorry, ladies. Where are my manners? Of course, I'll bring you both a towel. It's not every day I arrive home and find two beautiful young ladies dancing around in my swimming pool in their lingerie. I admit I was a little…distracted!' He stands up, walks back towards the villa and then glances back a couple of times. I can see his hair flopping back around.

As soon as he's out of sight, Steph and I are in fits of laughter again. I whisper, 'Oh my God. I thought he was a murderer!'

'I just thought he was a bloody perv!' says Steph. 'But what is he doing here? Does this mean we need to find somewhere else to stay?'

'Oh bugger, I hadn't thought of that. Hopefully it's just a misunderstanding – maybe a crossover in dates? Maybe he doesn't go home until tomorrow?'

'Hand over the wine please, babe. I need a swig to get over the shock!'

As I hand it over, he reappears in the doorway. 'Ladies, I shan't embarrass you any further. I'm so sorry, I didn't realise you were staying. I thought you were intruders, or I swear I would never have barged in on you like that! I'm going to leave you these towels on the table and take myself off to bed. Goodnight!'

'Goodnight,' we both call out as he walks back into the villa.

'There's a good chance he could still be a weirdo, you know!' Steph whispers making her way out of the pool. 'I'll keep lookout. You find your phone and text Lauren. I think we need to make sure he is her brother before we go waltzing into the house!'

'Very true. Although, I have to get into the kitchen to find my phone. If it's not there, he's most probably a murderer and he's taken it away so we can't call for help.'

'Don't be such a drama queen!' She rolls her eyes and helps me out of the pool. 'I'm sure it's all fine, but I just think we should check – you know, before we go to sleep in there for the night! Has she ever mentioned a brother?'

'No, but then she's quite a private person. She only really talks about Daddy because, you know, he owns the company. And her boyfriend, Richard.' I quickly run into the kitchen and grab my handbag. I run back out to Steph, pull my phone out of the bag and turn it on. Oops, I hadn't even switched it on after the flight. I've got messages pinging through from Mum wanting to know if we landed OK. Then one comes through from Lauren: *Oh gosh. I'm so sorry hon! My idiot brother has just text me! Hope you're ok and he didn't scare you! We have a family calendar and we're supposed to book out the villa. He obvs didn't bother to, so I didn't realise he would be there! Have a chat to him in the morning and let him/me know what you want to do x.*

I show the phone to Steph and then notice that she's already covered up. I pull my towel off the table and wrap it around me whilst she's reading it. This has got to be Egyptian cotton. I've heard my mum raving about that stuff being the best…and this is the best! It's the softest towel I've ever felt.

Steph hands the phone back. 'Party's over for tonight, then! Suppose we'd better find out where we're sleeping!'

'Oh yeah, more exploring!' We pick up all our things and take them back into the house, dumping anything we don't need on the kitchen island.

'Ames! Our cases have gone!' Steph whispers to me.

I walk into the hallway and realise that she's right. I look up and see them at the top of the staircase. 'There!' I announce, pointing to them. 'Maybe he took them up for us so we wouldn't have to struggle?'

'Maybe he's just a creep!' she replies.

We make our way upstairs barefoot, trying not to make any noise, but we're probably making a lot because we're so drunk and wobbly.

When we reach the top of the stairs, I look from left to right and see so many closed doors. 'How do we know which one?' I say to Steph.

'Only thing we can do is try 'em until we find what we need! Dunno about you, but I'm really hoping we find the toilet!' She giggles.

'Yeah, good point. I could really use the loo right now!' I say whilst opening the first door on the right just a crack. 'Jackpot. Bathroom.'

'Yesss!' Steph pushes past me, pulls her knickers down and sits straight on the loo.

I walk in, shut the door and pull the lock across. Even the bathroom is massive. There's a large double shower which looks like it has jets all around it, a huge Jacuzzi bath and a double sink.

'Shame they don't have two bloody toilets in here,' I grumble, crossing my legs. As soon as Steph flushes, I push her out of the way and plonk myself on the loo. 'Ahh, that's better!'

We both wash our hands and continue to search for a bed to sleep in. 'How many bedrooms has this place got exactly?' asks Steph.

'Erm, I think Lauren said five.'

'Right, the rest of these must be bedrooms then, eh?' She opens the door opposite the bathroom and flicks on the light. A lovely, simple bedroom in soft lilac colours. The bed is empty and all made up. 'This is me, then! Pass my case please, babe!' I wheel her case over slowly and gently, trying to be as quiet as I can. 'Cheers, hon. Night night, love ya.' She kisses me on each cheek and gently pulls the door closed.

I pull my case along and try the room next to hers. I'd like to stay close. Again, the room looks empty. There's a soft light coming through the window and I can just make out that the bed is made up. I'm too tired to bother turning the light on. I just want to go to bed now.

After bringing in my case and delicately closing the door behind me, I let the towel drop to the floor, pull my hair bobble out and run my fingers through my hair. I take off my damp underwear and pat myself dry with the towel. I'm so knackered that I can't be bothered to do my proper beauty regime. I can't even be bothered to get my PJs out of the case. The room is nice and cool; the air con must be on. I slip underneath the thin top sheet on the bed, bury my head in the super soft pillow and close my eyes.

CHAPTER SEVEN

A loud bang wakes me up. When I open my eyes, the sunlight is streaming through the windows. I sit up and take in my surroundings, figuring out where I am, and a smile spreads across my face. I can't wait to explore today. Ouch. Think I'm going to need some paracetamol first, though. My head is pounding. I really should have drunk some water in between all the wine last night! I make a mental note to self for next time.

I can feel the sheet across my whole body and realise that I'm naked. I try to remember my journey into bed. I see my case sat over by the door, unopened. My underwear is sat on top of it. Weird. Why did I do that? There's a big fluffy white towel folded up on a chair in the corner of the room. Oh yeah…the pool, the towel…the man. Oh shit, the man. Lauren's brother!

I scramble out of the bed in search of my phone. I don't find it, but there seems to be a lot of things in this room that don't belong to me. A wallet for one, on one of the bedside cabinets. On the dresser there's men's deodorant, aftershave, hair gel, even men's moisturiser. I open the wardrobe and it's full of men's clothes. I notice an en suite. I nudge the door open slightly. It's empty. Phew! I walk in and there's an electric toothbrush on charge, a tube of toothpaste on the sink and one solitary bottle of shower gel in the shower cubicle – more evidence that this is clearly a man's bathroom. So, obviously, I've ended up in Alex's bedroom; but for the life of me, I can't figure out why.

Realising that I'm strolling around his room naked, I run and grab my suitcase and leg it back into the en suite. I look in the mirror. I look terrible! My hair is matted and all over the place, I have mascara underneath my eyes like a panda, and my bloodshot eyes confirm that I had too much to drink last night.

I unzip my case, pull out my toiletries bag and get straight into the shower. I adjust the temperature so it's not burning my skin, and making me feel worse, and leave it on an almost too cold setting, which soothes my aching head as the cool water trickles over my hair and onto my face.

Whilst applying my array of toiletries, I try to piece together last night. I keep coming back to the same conclusion: I'm sure I got into an empty bed. Didn't he say he was going to bed? Surely *he* would have been in *his* bed? I don't remember neatly folding the towel or my underwear either. I'm ninety per cent sure I didn't. If I was sober enough to do that, why didn't I take off my make-up?

I finish rinsing my new fantastic conditioner out of my hair, turn off the shower and step out. I take a fluffy white towel off the rail and wrap it around me, taking a small one for my hair. I pull out some knickers, a T-shirt and a pair of shorts from my case, rip the tags off everything and quickly get dressed. I love wearing brand-new things.

After removing my make-up, brushing my teeth and towel-drying my hair, I take a long look in the mirror. Not too bad considering how I was looking twenty minutes ago. I dig around in my make-up bag and put in some cosmetic eye drops to take away the redness and some lip balm to make my lips shiny. If it were just Steph downstairs, I probably wouldn't have even had a shower yet. I'd have just thrown on a T-shirt and gone downstairs, but I have to make an effort because there's a boy in the house.

I shake my head at myself in the mirror. You'll do. I walk out of the bathroom and notice there's a balcony on the other side of the bed. I peek through the gap in the curtain and see the swimming pool area below. Alex is sat on a sunlounger reading a newspaper and drinking from a mug. I can't see much of him; his face is hidden behind the paper. I run out of the room to find Steph. As I close the bedroom door, I realise it's the noise that woke me up. The same heavy wooden door closing sound. Was he in there? While I was in there? I was naked! I knock gently on Steph's room. No answer. As I hover on the landing, I can smell food and hear clanging coming from the kitchen. She must be up already. I walk down the stairs, the floor cold beneath my feet.

'Hey, sleepyhead! Just in time!' calls Steph as she's plating up some beans on toast with grated cheese. 'Here's your hangover breakfast – you're welcome!' She winks and places it on the dining table. 'Alex has just showed me how to use the coffee machine. Want me to make you a latte?'

'Sounds amazing! Thanks!' I walk over to her and whisper, 'So, you've spoken to him, then?'

'Yeah, he seems quite nice. And hot to boot!' she says, mock fanning herself down. 'You are gonna love him!'

Once the coffee machine is on and making enough noise to hide my voice, I ask, 'Did he sleep in my room?'

She turns around straining to hear me. 'What?'

'Did he sleep in my room?' I ask again, too loudly this time as the coffee machine suddenly stops.

'I think you mean you slept in *my* room,' says a deep voice from behind.

Damn! I quickly turn around to face him, my cheeks flushed with embarrassment. 'Sorry,' I try to say, but the word hardly comes out at all, as I'm taken aback by his breathtaking appearance. He is hot. Too hot, in fact. Very well groomed. Not my type actually – he's too good-looking. Probably gay. All the good-looking ones are gay...aren't they? He has dark hair, piercing green eyes, bright white teeth and an amazing tan. 'Sorry,' I try again. 'I thought the bed was empty.'

'It was,' he replies. 'I was out on the balcony having a nightcap when I heard someone stumbling into my room. I was about to come in and inform you that it was my room, when you dropped your towel and proceeded to remove your underwear. I thought the gentlemanly thing to do was turn around. So, I sat back down and finished my drink. When I came into the room, you were already in the land of nod. Fast asleep!'

I hide my face behind my hands. This is majorly embarrassing. First my boss's brother finds me dancing in my underwear in the swimming pool. Then I strip in front him. 'I'm sooo sorry!' I say, hanging my head in shame.

Steph, on the other hand, is having a whale of a time. 'You didn't! Ha! That's hilarious!' She hands me my latte, and I shoot her a look that tells her to shut up. She presses her lips together trying her best to keep it in.

'I can't apologise enough. I'm so sorry!'

'It's fine. I found it all rather amusing, to be honest. I just thought I'd have some fun and wind you up a bit!' A crooked smile creeps across one side of his face, making a dimple appear in his cheek. It's so sexy.

I take a sip of my drink trying to take my mind off his mouth. Too hot! I don't want to make myself look like an idiot, so I just turn around swilling the coffee from side to side in my mouth.

'Well, I'll leave you ladies to enjoy your breakfast in peace. I'll be back in about an hour,' and with that, he's gone.

I finally swallow my coffee and turn around to face Steph just in time to see her burst into laughter. 'Oh my God, that could only happen to me!' I say, marching over to the table and sitting in front of my plate of food. My stomach grumbles in response and I tuck in.

Steph joins me at the table. 'He's a dish though, isn't he?' She wriggles her eyebrows up and down.

'He is *gorgeous*,' I agree. 'Gotta be gay though, hasn't he?'

'He's not gay, but I think he's taken. Heard him on the phone earlier to someone called Mia.' She makes a pouting face. 'Anyway, we got talking while we were waiting for you to get your lazy bum out of bed, and he is staying here for a while. He said he could probably find a hotel to put us up in, if we wanted, and he'd pay! Or, we could stay here. He said it's plenty big enough for us all to stay in. And he doesn't mind us being here, so long as we don't mind him being here. Oh, and we can help ourselves to all the food and wine. Which is good, coz we kinda already did!'

'What, you think we should just stay here with him?'

'Why not? The place is huge, and it's bloody amazing! I can't imagine a hotel would compare. Here, we have a pool to ourselves. We'd have to share with randoms if we went to a hotel.

And he's drop-dead gorge, even if he is taken – it makes for good eye candy!'

'Yeah, I suppose you're right. Well, I'm done. Thanks for breakfast. I really needed that!'

'No worries, hon. So, are we staying?' she asks with pleading eyes.

'Yeah, let's give it a go! If we feel it's not working later on, then we can check into a hotel. I'd best move all my stuff out of *his* room, then!'

'Yay! OK, I'll clear up down here. Meet you back downstairs in a bit and we can go check out the area?'

'Sure, sounds good to me.'

I find myself another bedroom, directly opposite Alex's, diagonally opposite Steph's and next door to the huge bathroom. It's about half the size of the others and there's no en suite, but there's a connecting door to the main bathroom, which is lockable from my side. I decide it will do. I don't fancy being too far away from everyone else. I hang up all my going-out outfits in the wardrobe and empty the rest of my things into the various drawers and cubbyholes.

I check out my reflection in the full-length mirror and decide I need to make more of an effort! I strip off, apply suntan lotion and rummage through a drawer for a bikini. I leave the white one; that will look so much better when I have a tan on this pasty body! I grab a blue one with orange flowers and try it on. Not looking too bad. I feel thinner. I suppose I have been skipping a few meals lately. My boobs look great in it actually, all pushed up. I find a blue skater dress to throw over the top, and I bling it up with some diamanté slip-on shoes and a long gold chain with a big heart on the end. I pull my hair into a ponytail and scrunch the ends.

And finally, I apply some waterproof mascara, a bit of green eyeliner that I bought from the MAC counter, which does wonders for my eyes, and apply MAC bronzer to my cheeks. I stand back and admire my handiwork. I grab my shades and bag and make my way downstairs, my shoes clip-clopping all the way down.

Steph is sitting outside on the rattan furniture. 'Ah, babe, you look great!' she says, handing me a bottle of water.

'Aw thanks, as do you!' I reply.

'So, is all this for Alex?'

'What, no, course not!'

'Good, because like I said, there's a Mia. And I'm sure there's plenty of nice-looking men outside this building. So, shall we head off?'

'Let's!'

As we walk out through the door, a black sporty-looking car pulls up on the driveway. Alex gets out, followed by a girl who I assume is Mia. She's pretty, very slim, with a short blonde bob and elegantly dressed, and she walks with attitude.

'Ladies! Off out adventuring?' asks Alex, striding towards us.

'Yeah, we're just gonna go check the place out. Get our bearings, ya know,' says Steph.

Mia walks straight past us and doesn't even look in our direction.

'So, you've decided to stay?' he asks, removing his expensive-looking sunglasses. His eyes dart from Steph to me; he gives me an intense stare. I feel my tummy flutter.

'Yeah, we're gonna stay, if you're sure that's OK?' says Steph.

'Absolutely! Lauren will be delighted.'

'Thanks for having us!' I pipe up, feeling like I should say something, but straight away I'm left feeling like an idiot.

He starts walking towards the house. As he passes me, he mutters, 'My pleasure.'

As we walk down the driveway, Steph links my arm. 'Thanks for having us!' She giggles.

'Argh, what's wrong with me? I'm such an idiot!'

'You're not an idiot! But you don't seem quite yourself around him. Still a bit freaked out he's seen you naked?'

'Well, maybe! And I don't know; my brain just turns to mush for some reason!'

'Oh girl, you've got it bad! He's got a *Mia*, remember. She was a bit of a bitch though, wasn't she – completely blanked us!'

'Yeah, I thought that was a bit strange. She's probably not very impressed that her boyfriend is shacked up with two random girls for the next nine days!'

'Two smoking hot random girls, you mean! I see your point!'

CHAPTER EIGHT

We walk along the promenade arm in arm, sussing out places that look nice to eat, which places do two-for-one cocktails, and wandering around the shops. We've been walking for a couple of hours and I'm starting to get thirsty.

'Shall we try out one of these bars?' I ask Steph.

She immediately drags me into the nearest bar. 'You read my mind! Ooh, let's sit here!' I notice she has strategically placed us by a table of men.

I casually try to check them out as if I'm looking at the blackboard behind advertising cocktail specials. I turn back to Steph. 'Not bad. A bit young maybe?'

'I'd say early twenties at a guess. Perfect for what you need, hon! We're not looking for your happily ever after. This is about getting you laid. Your Danny rebound! Oops, sorry, should not be mentioning his name!'

'No, you should not.' I take my phone out of my bag and answer Mum's messages, letting her know we're fine and that the place is lovely.

The waiter comes over, and Steph orders us both a mojito. I text Lauren to let her know we plan to stay and that the mix-up is not a problem. Our mojitos arrive. I was expecting it to be refreshing, but bloody hell it's strong. I forgot about holiday alcohol measures being twice what we'd get back home. I'm hardly struggling to drink it, though; it's half gone already. I see Steph signal to the waiter. She orders two more.

'Erm, maybe we should get a bit of food for soakage? Share a bowl of chips or something?'

'Ooh! Look at you being all sensible, Ames! You're right, though. It's a bit early to be getting trollied, isn't it? I'll go ask them for some.' As she walks back over to the table, she gets a wolf whistle from the table of guys. She smiles and sits back down. 'This is going to be easier than I thought!' and she gives them a wave.

'What are you doing? I can't believe you just waved at them!'

'Shh...incoming!'

I look up to see two of them making their way over to our table.

'Alright?' one of them asks. He's not bad looking; he just looks so young. He's a bit lanky and has a shaved head, but you can see he's naturally dark haired. He's wearing a vest top showing off his large muscles. He introduces himself to Steph as Paul.

'I'm Shaun,' says the other lad to me. He's alright looking too. Young again. He's a bit weedier looking. He has blond wavy hair and blue eyes, and looks a bit like a surfer.

'Hi, I'm Amy.' I shake his hand.

Paul seems to be working his charms on Steph.

'So, what are you girls up to tonight?' Shaun asks me.

'We're not sure yet. We only got here late last night.'

'Well, how about we show you girls a great bar? They give out free shots all the time. It's totally crazy in there and they play some banging tunes!' Shaun has got quite a nice smile.

'Sounds good to me. Steph?' I ask, cutting into their conversation. 'Fancy meeting these guys later, they know a good bar?'

'Yeah sure, hon. Sounds awesome.'

'That's a yes, then!' I say to Shaun. The second round of cocktails arrive along with our bowl of chips.

'Oh, we best leave you to your lunch!' says Paul.

'Not before we get your digits, though!' Shaun says, looking at me.

'Well, I have my phone here. Why don't you put your number in and we'll message you later?' I unlock the screen and hand over my phone; he taps away rapidly and hands it back.

'See ya later, then!' says Shaun.

'See you, beautiful,' Paul says to Steph, and they make their way back over to all their mates. They're greeted with cheering and clapping, and one of them grabs his crotch and rocks his hips back and forth.

I look at Steph. 'What on earth have we just let ourselves in for?'

'Boys will be boys! When there's a big group like that, it can't be helped. They're on a stag do, Paul said.'

'Bit young to be getting hitched already! Reckon he got her up the duff?'

'Huh! Probably!'

I look at my phone and see that he's entered his name as 'Sexy Shaun'. I show it to Steph. 'The cheek of it!'

'They're confident, that's for sure! Young and cocky. Perfect rebound material!'

'What's your excuse, then? You're not on a rebound!'

'I am having some well-earned fun!' she says. 'Now shut it and scoff some of these chips before I eat them all!'

We get back to the villa and spend the afternoon sunbathing around the pool and drinking a couple of beers we picked up on the way back. Alex wasn't in. I realised I was a bit gutted about that. I keep my sexiest sunbathing pose going, just in case he comes back.

Steph sits up. 'Well, I suppose we'd better start getting ready soon. It's half six already. How long is it going to take you to beautify yourself, Ames?'

'At least an hour. Actually, make that an hour and a half. I was going to straighten my hair.'

'Cool, let's go make a start, then. You'd better text the boys and see what time we need to meet.'

I find my phone where I dumped it on the kitchen island. I type a message to Shaun: *Hiya, it's Amy. What's the plan later?* 'Kiss or no kiss?' I ask Steph.

'You have to put a kiss. How will he know if you're flirting otherwise?'

'OK.' I add a kiss at the end and press send.

We don't have to wait long before there's a reply: *Hey u! Meet*

@ Charlie's bar @ 9ish.

I look up at Steph. 'No kiss!' I'm furious I put a kiss and he didn't. 'That makes me look *needy*! Like I'm chasing after him! And it was blatantly him cracking on to me! And what does he mean, hey *you*? Bloody *you*?'

'Calm down, babe! You can't read that much into a text message! You're overthinking it!'

'Where the bloody hell is Charlie's bar anyway?'

'That's the name of the bar we were in earlier. We might need to get a taxi. I don't think I can walk that far in heels!'

'Good call. I'll be a big sweaty mess by the time I've walked all the way down there! We better hurry, then. I take it we'll eat before we meet them?'

'Ooh yeah. How about the Chinese place? If we get a taxi there, we only have a ten-minute walk to meet them.'

'Sounds like a plan, Batman!' I chuck my phone back onto the kitchen island and go upstairs to get ready.

I'm showered (for the second time today), my hair is dry and my make-up is on. I'm wearing a cute little pink playsuit, which I dress up with heels and chunky jewellery. I hope it makes me look great, but not like I've tried to make too much of an effort. I want this Shaun to think I look good. I don't want him to think I've put in a lot of effort just for *him*! He's cocky enough; he doesn't need any more encouragement. I spray a couple of squirts of my new perfume and go over to Steph's room to use the straighteners. I knock on, and she opens the door in her underwear and lets me in.

'You look nice, babe.'

'Thanks. How come you're not dressed yet? Are the straighteners ready?'

'Yeah, help yourself. I've finished with them. I just wanted your opinion. Long turquoise maxi dress? Or short red dress?'

'Well, as I've got my legs out, you know full well I'm going to tell you to wear the short red one!'

'Red it is!' She slips it over her head and starts applying more eyeshadow.

I'm starting to regret straightening my hair. It does it easy enough, but the frizz! 'Steph, this is not the right humidity to try and make my wavy hair straight! Help!'

'Oh,' she says, turning to look at me. 'Here, use this serum, always works for me,' and she turns back to the mirror.

I get a dollop in my hands and rub it all through my hair. 'Erm, is it supposed to do this? I look like a greaseball!'

'Ooh...you only needed a tiny amount, hon. How much did you put in?'

'Too much, obvs! Great, what am I supposed to do now?'

'Here, we'll fix it, don't stress.' She tries combing it out, getting the hairdryer on it, even dry shampooing it. It looks better than it did, but I've ruined my chances of wearing it down. She gets it into a high ponytail and with a bit of backcombing, it doesn't look like I haven't washed it for a week any more.

'Thanks, hon, you're a lifesaver.' I throw my arms around her and kiss her on the cheek.

'Ladies!' It's Alex. I open the door, and he's at the bottom of the stairs waving my phone towards us. 'Sexy Shaun is trying to reach you!' he says with an amused face.

Shit. How do I keep embarrassing myself in front of this man! I walk down the stairs and take the phone from him trying to avoid eye contact. 'Thanks.' I walk into the lounge and pick up. 'Hello?'

'Hey! Change of plans, sorry. Can you meet us straight at the bar I was telling you about?'

'The crazy one with the shots?'

'Yeah. It's called Bar Loco. It's not that far from Charlie's.'

'Bar Loco. OK, see you there.'

'Bye, baby!'

I put the phone down. Baby! Please. I'm not your baby. I'm not even sure why I've agreed to this. Going to meet a group of strange men in a bar. I'd never agree to this back home! Being on holiday makes you friendlier, I guess. You speak to all sorts of people you'd likely just ignore if you were still in the UK. Why the sudden change of plan anyway? I turn around and Alex is standing in the doorway looking at me.

'Is everything OK, Amy?'

'Yeah, fine,' I say quickly. I realise I've been standing here probably with an annoyed look on my face. It's nice of him to be concerned.

'So, is *sexy* Shaun a jealous boyfriend you've left at home?'

'Absolutely not! He's someone I met just today actually.'

'Oh, wow! Fast mover!'

'*I* didn't put his name as that in my phone, by the way! *He* did that! He just said he would show us a cool place to go for a drink later, that's all.'

'Oh right. Sounds like a real gent!' he says before turning to walk away.

'Did you fold up my underwear?' I blurt out.

He slowly turns back around, and for once he's the one to be embarrassed. 'Erm, yeah. I'm sorry about that. I was walking past it on my way out after I discovered you comatose in my bed. I didn't want to walk all over it. I thought afterwards I probably shouldn't have done that. I do apologise.'

'No, it's fine. I probably shouldn't have been naked in your bed!'

'Well, I have no complaints about that, I can assure you.'

I look at the floor biting my lip. I can't figure out if he's flirting with me or if he's just extremely polite. He does seem very over polite about everything. 'Oh, and were you in the room, in the morning? Only I heard the door close?'

'Guilty again. Sorry, Amy. I just popped my head in to see if I could come back in, but you were still in there. So I just wore clothes from the day before to come down in.'

'Oh, course, all your stuff was in there. Sorry!' I feel a bit disheartened. I was reading too much into it. I thought maybe he had picked up my underwear to admire it and he'd come into the room just to see me. 'I'd better go check if she's ready yet. If

I leave her to her own devices, she'll spend half the night apply-ing more make-up!' I walk past him to get to the stairs and hear him take a deep breath.

'You smell incredible, by the way.'

'I do?'

'Mmm.' God, that sound coming from him sounds so sexy. 'And you made my bed sheets have that same incredible smell.'

'Thank you, new perfume,' I say as I turn and strut up the stairs with a large grin on my face. That new perfume was one hundred per cent worth it! I hope he's watching me walk up the stairs. I'm putting on my sexiest walk. It takes everything I have not to turn around and check if he's watching. I can't get the ri-diculous big grin off my face!

CHAPTER NINE

We finish our Chinese meal and I am stuffed. 'That was yummy, Steph. Good choice! But I'm not sure I can move now!'

'Ah, I know. I think we need a cocktail to wash it down for pudding! What d'ya reckon?'

'I think I could use a drink for sure before we meet those guys!'

'Not nervous, are we?' she asks, getting the waiter's attention. She orders us both a tequila sunrise. 'A nice fruity long drink, easy to drink after a massive meal,' she explains, 'and the tequila is for your nerves!'

'I'm not nervous because I'm really into him. I'm nervous because we've agreed to meet a large group of strange men!'

'It's just a bit fun, babe. We're only going to a bar! Nothing bad will happen, I promise.' Steph has always been one for chatting to guys and getting free drinks out of them. I'm the cautious one who worries they're plying her with free drinks because they've spiked them, and I have to 'accidently' knock them over.

The drinks arrive and we ask for the bill. A text comes through from Shaun: *Hey, where r u girls at...not standin us up, are ya? X.* I show the phone to Steph.

'A kiss! He gave you a kiss! Well, he's obviously the type you have to treat mean to keep him keen. We're late meeting them, made no contact, and suddenly he's insecure and trying to make sure he still has you on his hook.'

'Well, he can wait some more,' I say, putting the phone back into my bag without replying. We finish our drinks, pay the bill and head straight to the ladies to freshen up.

Bar Loco is not hard to spot. It's on a corner, it looks packed, and you can hear the music blasting from three bars down. That must piss the other bars off. There's a white wall around the perimeter, full of drunk people sitting on it, shouting, cheering and generally spilling their drinks all over the place.

'Blimey, this place really draws a crowd!' Steph shouts, leading me through the masses by my hand.

As we reach the bar, I can hear someone whistling really loudly. I turn and see Paul standing on a table.

He waves at us, jumps down and barges people out of the way to get to us. He greets me with a hug. 'Alright?'

'Hi!' I reply.

He then pulls Steph towards him and goes straight in for a kiss. She puts her hand on his chest to push him away and leans her head backwards to avoid it. 'You think you can get a kiss without buying a lady a drink first?' she shouts over the thumping music.

'Right! Sorry, my bad! What do you girls want to drink?'

'G and T?' she asks, turning to face me.

I nod in agreement. It's so bloody loud in here.

After a few minutes he comes back, hands me my drink and points towards the table he jumped off.

'Thanks,' I try and shout to him. I head towards the table of men; they all look totally wasted. I spot Shaun sat at the other end of the table talking to some other girl. She's obviously really into him; I can practically see her eyelashes fluttering from here. He looks like he's flirting, too, smiling his nice easy smile and running his hand through his hair. I kept him waiting too long. He's moved on. I turn to look for Steph and see Paul snogging her face off. They look so into each other, like they're going to start ripping each other's clothes off at any moment. Jeez, get a room. Great, I'm left standing here like a spare bloody wheel.

Suddenly, there's a loud claxon sound and the whole bar starts going crazy. Everyone's jumping up and down on the spot making *choo-choo* sounds and pumping their fists in the air as though pulling an imaginary train horn. What on earth is going on?

Then I spot some beautiful, very scantily clad ladies making their way through the crowd. They are placing trays full of shots on each table. They also have a bottle in their hands. People are bending down open-mouthed, and they're pouring it straight into their mouths. I notice one of those people is Steph. I can't help but giggle. She's such a party animal. So, that explains why it's known as the crazy shot place.

One of the girls approaches me. 'Hola! Si! Si!' she yells, and I shake my head. Next thing I know, she's pulling my ponytail. As my head tips backwards, she holds the bottle over and begins to pour. I open my mouth and swig whatever it is, because it's a better option than it dribbling all down my face. 'Si! Si!' she cheers, clapping me and smiling.

There's a slight burning sensation and a strong aniseed flavour. Sambuca, I realise. It could have been worse; I quite like sambuca. I wipe the residue from my lips as I feel a hand around my waist. I turn to see Shaun.

'Impressive!' he says. 'A girl who can take her drink! I like it!'

'What about the girl you were just with?' I ask a bit aggressively.

'Who her? She's no one, darlin'. Not getting jealous, are ya?'

'What? No! I just… I don't want to keep you from her, that's all.'

'Ha, she's got nothin' on you, babe. Come here!' and he pulls me towards him. He goes straight in for a full-on snog, and although it's hard and fast and not how I'm used to kissing, I have to admit it feels quite exciting. It's nice to have the attention from someone who is keen and clearly thinks I'm attractive. It's the ego boost I needed.

The drinks keep flowing and Steph and I have been having a good dance, in the little space we have available, on the table mostly! The lads break us up for what seems like a snogathon every now and then, and we have to keep prising ourselves away to come up for air so we can have a dance.

I realise it's on the hour every hour that the shot train of girls come out and do their thing. I am feeling so drunk and starting to get tired. My feet are hurting from all the dancing. I turn to Steph. 'Shall we make a move? I think I'm ready for bed!'

'Actually, if it's OK with you, I might go back with Paul first, and then meet you back at the villa later?'

'Steph, are you sure? You've only just met this guy!'

'It's been a few months since I got me some, babe, and I'm on to a sure thing here,' she slurs.

'Yeah, but you've had a lot to drink, and you don't know him well enough!'

'I appreciate you looking out for me, but I'm a big girl, Amy! I can look after myself. Here, give me your phone.' I hand it to her. After about five minutes, she gives it back. 'There, you just need to go on Find My Phone and you can see where I am. His hotel is just around the corner. I'll meet you back at our place in a couple of hours. OK, beaut?'

'Fine, if you insist, but I don't like this!'

'Thanks, babe!' She wraps her arms around the back of my head, pulling my face into her chest in a drunken hug. She kisses the top of my head and walks over to Paul. I see them holding hands on their way out. I'm left standing there stunned. I can't believe she actually just did that. I feel pretty sober now. A serious situation does that to you sometimes, doesn't it?

Shaun pulls me over and practically throws me against the wall. The club is emptying now; it must be near closing. His forceful kisses no longer feel like harmless fun as they did earlier.

'Stop,' I say, trying to push him away, but he just presses harder against me, his hips leaning me back into the wall. 'STOP!' I shout as I start to panic.

'What's the matter?' he asks. The kissing has stopped, but I'm still pinned against the wall. I'm getting a flashback of Danny, when he had me up against the wall in his flat, and how it made me feel so used and disgusting. 'I'm ready to go now,' I say.

'Awesome! Let's get back to the hotel!'

'No, I mean I want go back my place.'

'Sweet. Anywhere is good with me!'

'No, you're not getting it! You go home and I'll go home. OK?'

His smile disappears and his face goes dark. 'You fuckin bitch!' he spits out. 'You're just a tease! Looks like I chose the wrong one! It's just my luck to get the frigid one!' The change from happy-go-lucky to moody is instant.

'Excuse me! What did you just call me?' I shout back at him. I'm shocked and I think the alcohol is giving me a false sense of confidence.

'You heard me!' he sneers.

'Amy!' someone calls.

I look over trying to locate the voice. Alex is coming towards us! He looks at me. Realising I have tears on my cheeks, I dab at them with the back of my hands.

'I think you'd better leave!' he says to Shaun.

'Yeah, whatever. I'm going, pal,' he says, backing away.

'What...what are you doing here, Alex?'

'I'm just in the right place at the right time, by the looks of it. Do you want a lift back to the villa?'

'That'd be great, thanks!'

He opens the passenger door of his little black sports car and helps me in. Very chivalrous. He gets in the driver's side and then helps me with my seat belt – as I appear to be too drunk or just crying too much to operate it. He opens the glovebox and hands me a packet of tissues. 'You wanna talk about it?'

'No,' I say, pressing the tissue into my eyes, trying to force the tears back.

He pulls up outside the villa and undoes both of our seat belts. He gets out, walks around to my side and holds out his hand to help me from the car. A good job really, as I don't think I'd be able to get out of this low sporty seat in a very ladylike manner.

We go inside, and he sits me down on the sofa in the lounge. 'I'll get you a coffee. Latte, isn't it?'

'That'd be lovely, thanks. Yes, latte please.' While he's in the kitchen, I pull my mirror out of my bag. I wipe my eyes, smooth my hair and powder the shine away from my face. When I hear the coffee machine stop, I quickly put everything back in my bag and place it on the floor.

He walks in and stops in the doorway. He has two mugs in his hand, but he's just staring down at me. He takes a breath and walks the rest of the way, placing the cups on the table and sitting down next to me. 'What did that idiot do to you?'

'Nothing,' I reply.

'It wasn't nothing!' He seems angry now. I've only ever seen him with an amused expression, usually laughing at my expense! Now his mouth is set in a tight line and I can see the muscles in his jaw tightening. 'Sexy Shaun, I assume?'

'Yeah, that was him,' I say, looking down at my lap. 'Look, he tried it on, but nothing happened. He just didn't like being told no for an answer, that's all.'

'I gathered that much,' he says and picks up a mug, handing it to me. 'Here, drink,' he orders.

I take it from him and have a sip. 'Thank you. For being my knight in shining armour and rescuing me.' I look at him, and his bright green eyes are staring right into me again. I have to remind myself to breathe.

'You're most welcome. I do love to save a damsel in distress.' He smiles. His low voice is soft and soothing. I feel safe now, back here with him. 'So, you lost Steph?'

'Yeah, she went off with someone. I can't believe she did that! I hope she's alright. Knowing what his friend is like makes me worry all the more for her.'

'We can go and find her if you like?'

'I can find her on an app on my phone by searching her phone location if I need to. If she's not back in an hour though, I might take you up on that.'

'Of course, no worries.' We sit and drink our coffee in silence while my mind is now running riot worrying about Steph and coming up with completely irrational and unlikely scenarios.

We lean over to the table to put our mugs down at the same time, our heads nearly bumping into each other. 'Sorry,' we both say at the same time, but we don't move away.

He tilts his head towards me slightly, and I'm sure he's about to try and kiss me. Then he pulls back and exhales a slow steady stream of air as he straightens himself up. I sit back up feeling gutted. I totally misread that situation. Why would he want to kiss me anyway? I'm such a fool.

I then hear Steph stumbling in through the front door. 'Thank God!' I shout and run to the door. 'Hey, you OK?'

'Yeah fine, babe! You all good? Told you I'd be back! True to my word, aren't I!'

'So, you had a nice time?'

'I don't think *nice* is the word I'd use!' she begins. 'More like hot and steamy...' She trails off as Alex walks into the hallway and she giggles. 'Er...I'll fill you in on the details tomorrow, babe, yeah? I'm just gonna grab a water and get to bed.'

'Good idea.' I laugh. 'Grab me a bottle, please?'

'Sure!'

'I'm glad she's OK,' Alex says to me. 'Goodnight.'

'Me too. Thanks again, for earlier. Night.'

'Night, Alex!' calls Steph, and she clambers up the stairs with our water.

I run up to steady her, scared she's going to fall back down them. I look at Alex with a 'help me' expression, but he's standing there shaking his head and smiling.

Steph goes into her room and hands me my water. 'Night, babe. Love ya!'

'Night. Love ya!' I call back.

CHAPTER TEN

I lie awake the next morning thinking about Alex. I can't stop thinking about that almost kiss moment. I should not even be thinking like this. He has a girlfriend; I need to snap out of it.

There's a knock on the door. 'Ames, you awake?'

'Come in, Steph.'

She walks into the room looking sheepish. 'I'm so sorry about last night, babe!'

'You had me worried the whole time you were gone!'

She creeps into my bed and snuggles up to me sticking her bottom lip out and looking at me with her big puppy dog eyes.

'Come here!' I admit defeat and wrap my arms around her. I can't stay mad at this woman. 'Feeling a little worse for wear, are we?' I ask.

'Yeah. My turn to be dying of a hangover today,' she croaks.

'I'll make us breakfast. You go and get showered.'

'Ah, you're the best, Ames. Thanks, babe!'

'Can I just ask something about last night?'

'Sure, what's up?'

I get out of bed and run my hands through my hair trying to think how to ask her. 'Paul. He didn't...he didn't hurt you, did he?'

'What? Course not! Why would you ask that? Oh my God. Did Shaun hurt you? Are you OK? What did he do?' She bolts up off the bed and moves my face around, inspecting me for damage.

I push her hands away. 'No, he didn't, don't worry. But he looked like he might, at one point. You had gone off with Paul already, then he was trying to get me to go back to his hotel, but I didn't want to. I didn't want to go, Steph!'

'Heyyy, it's OK. Come here, shh.' She pulls me in for a hug and starts rocking me. 'Tell me what happened.'

'Well, I said I wanted to go. He said great let's go. I kinda said not with you – I just wanna go! And he changed. He went from happy drunk to moody drunk, just like that! Called me a frigid bitch, basically!'

'OMG, babe. I can't believe he did that! What a dick! Then what happened?'

'Then Alex appeared, out of nowhere. It was really random. He told Shaun to leave me alone.'

'Alex?'

'Yeah, and he brought me back, and we had coffee, and then eventually you came back.'

She climbs back into the bed. 'Well, I'm so glad you're OK and that Alex was there. I feel even more shitty now. I'm so sorry I left you with that jerk!'

'Don't worry. I'm gonna go get brekkie on.'

Alex comes into the kitchen. 'Something smells good!' His voice makes me both jump and my tummy flutter all at same time.

'Pancakes! Want some?' I ask, trying to be all nonchalant.

'Yes, I'd love some. Thank you. How are you this morning?'

'I'm OK. I'd rather not go over it all again, if that's OK. I'm trying to put it to the back of my mind and not let it ruin my holiday.'

'Sure, whatever you want.' He sits at the dining table, and I feel him watching my every move.

Steph walks in. 'Ahh pancakes! Is it Pancake Day?'

'No, Pancake Day is in February,' I inform her.

'Oh, I only ever usually have pancakes on Pancake Day. Don't know why. They're really nice! Oh, morning, Alex!' She sits down opposite him.

'Good morning, Stephanie. I have to say, you're not looking too bad, considering the state you rolled back in last night!'

'Why thank you!' she says, taking the compliment and completely ignoring the insult.

I set the pancakes down on the middle of the table and sit

next to Steph and we all start tucking in.

'Amy, I've been speaking to Paul, and he said Shaun is really sorry and that he's been texting you,' says Steph.

Alex drops his fork. 'And that makes it alright then does it, excuses his behaviour?'

'Well, no, I didn't say that. But you know, he's trying to apologise. He just had too much to drink.'

'Having too much to drink doesn't give someone a free pass to be atrocious. It's not a "get out of jail free" card!' With that, he leaves the table.

'What was *that* about?' she asks, turning to me.

'I'm not sure about the storming off bit...but he has a point about the rest of it really. Are you asking me to forgive him? Is this because you want to hang out with Paul all holiday now and it's going to make things awkward for you if I don't get on with his mate?'

'No, babe, not at all! I'm here on holiday to spend time with you! I'm not bothered if I don't see him ever again!'

'Good. Can we just have a day at the beach and relax today then, please? We've had so much to drink the last couple of days; I think I just fancy taking it easy.'

'Course, babe, sounds ace! The pancakes are so good by the way! Thank you!'

'No worries. I'm gonna go and get ready.'

She's right, I have nine text messages from him. I don't even read them; I just delete them all. I block his number and delete it from my contacts. Now it's time to forget about him and move on. I'm ready to go to the beach. I finish packing my bag and walk downstairs. Alex is sitting in the lounge.

'I'm sorry about earlier, Amy,' he says.

'That's OK. You were just sticking up for me.'

'I shouldn't have flown off the handle like that. Stephanie didn't deserve it.'

'So, apologise to me, then.' Steph appears in the doorway.

'I'm sorry, Stephanie,' says Alex. 'I know it's not my place to interfere, I hardly even know either of you, but from where I was stood, he looked like he was going to hurt Amy. I just don't want you to hang out with those creeps again. Besides, Lauren would kill me if anything happened to you!'

'That's OK. I actually think it's quite sweet that you're looking out for her. We won't hang out with them again – promise! We're going to the beach now if you wanna join us?'

'Oh, thanks. I have to meet Mia now, but I might pop down to the beach later. Maybe see you there?'

'Maybe! Come on, Ames, let's go.'

As we walk out, Alex hands me a business card. 'My number, in case you find yourself in any trouble again,' he explains.

'Oh, thanks. I try not to make a habit out of the whole damsel routine! But thanks, that's really nice of you.'

'No problem.'

The beach is gorgeous. Light green sea, proper sand. I hate shingle; it always spoils a beach for me. You go into the sea and come out with a load of stones in your foo foo. Ew! We've been lying here for a couple of hours now, and all I can think about is Alex.

'Do you think he likes me?' I ask Steph.

She looks up from her magazine. 'Huh?'

'Alex, do you think he likes me?'

'Course he does!' she says and goes back to reading celebrity gossip.

'No, I mean *likes me*, likes me?'

'Oh, I don't know. Why, has something happened?'

'No, nothing's happened. Well, last night I thought he might kiss me, but he didn't. I can't work out if he's into me or if he's just really polite! It's hard to tell. He's quite well-spoken, isn't he? Maybe he's just being nice to me because of Lauren.'

'What about Mia? I mean, he seems lovely, and he's hot, but you've been messed around by the guy who we can no longer mention whose name begins with D, and you got messed about with by that div last night. I just don't want you to get involved with someone who has a girlfriend and you end up hurt again.'

'I know, you're right. I should leave him well alone.'

Steph pulls her phone out of her bag. 'It's Paul again. He keeps messaging me asking to meet up again. Don't worry, I set him straight, told him it ain't gonna happen.'

'Do you want to see him again? I feel a bit bad banning you from seeing him just because his mate wasn't nice to me.'

'Don't be daft. I'm here to holiday with you!' she says, swatting me with the magazine.

'You never finished telling me about your drunken escapade. You stopped at hot and steamy, I believe, when Alex walked in!'

'Oh, I forgot about that! Well, it was hot and steamy. I hit the nail on the head there.' She looks dreamily into the distance. 'What can I say? I know he's a bit rough and ready, probably not boyfriend material, but he was just what I needed last night. He has stamina!' she says, looking at me, her face all lit up.

'You can see him again, if you want? I'm not going to go with you, though. Why don't you see if you can get him away from his cronies later and meet him for round two?'

'No, I couldn't do that to you, babe!'

'It's fine, honestly. I'm feeling a chilled one tonight. After two heavy nights partying with you…I think you've broke me! I'll be quite happy to sit in the villa and read, maybe watch a film.'

'Well, if you're absolutely sure? I wouldn't mind a round two in all honesty. I think I was too drunk to appreciate it properly last night!'

'What are you like?' I laugh. 'Yeah, it's fine, go for it!'

'OK, I'll text him. Thanks, hon!'

Alex then comes strolling over with three bottles of beer. Yes! I've got him to see me in my sunbathing pose. I hope I'm looking as sexy as I'm trying to look. A little voice in the back of my head is screaming, '*Mia!*' I try my hardest to push it to the back of my mind. He hands us a bottle each.

'Good afternoon, ladies!'

'Aw thanks! Here, sit.' I swing my legs off the sunlounger and sit up to make room for him.

After downing half the bottle of beer, Steph says, 'Ahh! Thanks, this is just what I needed! A bit of hair of the dog!'

'Ha, I thought it might go down well. You're looking a bit sunburnt, Amy, just on your nose and your shoulders.'

'Oh, thanks, I didn't notice I was burning.' So much for looking sexy. All he's noticed is that I look like a beetroot! Steph's right, I'm wasting my time on this one. He's clearly not interested. *'Because he already has a girlfriend,'* says that same annoying voice. I take the sun cream out of my bag and start to reapply.

As soon as I start rubbing it into my chest, Alex stands up. 'I'm just going to have a quick dip.' He then takes off his T-shirt.

Oh. My. God. This is the first time I've seen him not wearing a top. His body is amazing. All muscly and chiselled, not too much hair on his chest, just a little sprinkle…and that sexy hairline that leads straight into his shorts. I realised I've stopped rubbing cream and I'm just staring at him like a gawping idiot. He doesn't seem to notice.

As soon as he's put his beer down and thrown his wallet on the bed out of his shorts pocket, he strolls straight towards the sea. I watch in awe until he reaches the water and dives in. I turn to Steph still open-mouthed with a chest full of sun cream. My hands seem to have lost all ability to continue what they were doing.

Steph says, 'OMG! He's a right bloody Adonis isn't he!'

'Adonis,' I agree, staring at the sea waiting for him to pop up again.

'Earth to Amy!' Steph laughs while clicking her fingers in front of me.

'Sorry!' I say, snapping out of it. I carry on rubbing in the cream.

'Well, he's very trusting. He's just thrown his wallet next to you. He's only known us a couple of days.' Steph points at the wallet on the end of the lounger.

'Maybe he's just a good judge of character? Oh plus, I woke up next to his wallet once. Probably figured I didn't take anything that time, so I won't this time. His family are that rich, I bet he wouldn't miss any money anyway! Oh, showtime, hon, twelve o'clock!' I nod towards the sea, and we watch him and his glorious body coming out dripping wet. 'It's just like the James Bond scene,' I pant.

'Or the Diet Coke advert,' suggests Steph.

CHAPTER ELEVEN

We're back at the villa. Alex has gone out to meet Mia, and Steph is getting ready to meet Paul. She assured me that she is only meeting Paul, none of his friends. I'm quite looking forward to a night in alone. I've got a pizza ordered for my dinner thanks to Alex before he left. He spoke fluent Spanish on the phone to the restaurant, it was so sexy!

I sit myself down on the rattan furniture and enjoy the evening breeze while I read my book. I have to keep rereading parts when my mind wanders to Alex, because I realise I haven't absorbed what I've just read at all. Steph comes outside. She's gone for the turquoise maxi dress today.

'You look great, Steph!'

'Thanks! You really sure you don't mind? Because if you do, I'll drop him like a hot cake for you, babe. You know that, right?'

'I know, apart from last night!' I say, laughing, although there's truth in it. I'm still quite pissed at her for going off with him.

'Aw, I'm so sorry. You know what I'm like when I've had too much to drink! I get something in my head and that's it – I'm determined to see my plan through!'

'I know,' I say, 'you're like a dog with a frigging bone! Just don't drink too much tonight, hey? I don't want to be worrying about you all night.'

'OMG, I'm never drinking that much ever again, trust me! That place was crazy, wasn't it? I can't believe they just give out free shots all the time!'

'I know, quite clever though, isn't it?' I ponder. 'They started off the night with strong shots – sambuca, tequila – and by the end of the night it was peach schnapps and apple sours. It was packed, so the free shots obviously draw everyone in. Then, because everyone is wasted, they spend loads of money on all those fancy gins. They were fifteen euros a pop!' I look at Steph. Her face is turning the same colour as her dress. 'You OK?' I ask.

'I was getting through my hangover OK until you just listed every drink I had last night. *Urgh*. The thought of tequila is making me feel quite sick!'

'Sorry, honey! God, no wonder you were smashed! As soon as I saw those shot women heading my way, I picked up an empty glass off the table and kept it in my hand!' I giggle.

'Oh, so they thought you already had one, you clever girl!'

'Thanks!' I grin. 'It's also the reason why I know everything that you consumed. I got the waft from the empty glasses. If I'd drunk all those, I'd have puked!'

We are suddenly interrupted by the doorbell.

'Yay! My pizza!' I cheer as I get up and run to the door. The delivery man is standing there with three pizzas. Hmm, I only ordered one. I'm too polite to argue, so I just ask him how much. He hands them over and waves his hand shouting that it's paid for and to enjoy. Well, I'm not going to argue with that! I hurry to the kitchen to chuck them on the island because the heat is beginning to burn my arms.

'They smell amazing,' says Steph as she enters the kitchen.

'Don't they! I don't know how we ended up with three pizzas, or why we got them for free,' I say while opening each box to see what delights await. There's a pepperoni one with jalapeños, a plain cheese and tomato, and a veggie one. Perfect.

'Alex must have paid?' says Steph. 'Save me some for later. I'm off now. Enjoy your film!' She kisses me on each cheek.

'Enjoy your hot, steamy sex!' I call after her.

Four slices of pizza and two chapters of my book later, I decide to go for a bath. I've been dying to try this Jacuzzi contraption out! I grab a bottle of beer and my book, strip off in my room and go through the adjoining door straight into the bathroom. I fill the bath with water only. I've heard that bubbles in a Jacuzzi are a recipe for disaster.

Once I'm in, I press the on button and it whirrs into life. This is ace! I grab my book and beer and sit blissfully relaxing for about ten minutes. After the novelty has worn off, as it's just too noisy, I turn the bubbles off. I'd rather just relax in the peace and quiet.

After placing down my book and beer, I sink my head under the water for a few seconds. As I sit myself up, the door opens and Alex walks in. We stare at each other for a few seconds before he runs back out and shouts an apology. Shit! Because I entered the bathroom through my room, I completely forgot to lock the main bathroom door! I wasn't expecting him back so soon.

I climb out, grab my things and a towel and go into my room. I throw on a pyjama vest and short set and pluck up the courage to face him. I walk downstairs and into the kitchen where he's leaning over the counter holding his head in his hands.

'I'm so sorry, Amy!' he says without turning to look at me.

Am I that hideous? Have I scarred him for life? 'No, I'm sorry, Alex. I completely forgot to lock the door because I went in through the bedroom! You have nothing to be sorry about! Pizza?' I ask, trying to lighten the mood and move past the fact that I keep showing far too much of my body to this man!

He turns to face me. 'You're so forgiving, thank you. And I would love some pizza, thanks.'

'I believe I should be thanking you! I didn't have to pay and there was triple what I ordered!'

'Ha, yeah. It's fine, I sorted it. And I might have ordered extra in the hope there would be some left for you to share with me?'

I smile. Is that flirting? He makes it really difficult for me to figure out. 'What happened to seeing Mia?' I ask him.

'I saw her,' he replies, shrugging his shoulders.

'You weren't gone very long?'

'Long enough,' he says, staring at me with those beautiful eyes of his.

'Want to eat while watching a film?' I ask, hopeful.

'Sounds great.'

I've had the best evening. We put on a comedy and we've both been howling with laughter. I found that we get on really well – we just seem to bounce off each other. We've never been this relaxed around each other before. I'm sitting in my PJs, hair scraped up and piled on top of my head and no make-up. Maybe it's because I'm au naturel, I've taken the pressure off myself trying to be attractive for him.

'What is it you do then anyway?' I ask. 'Because you don't work at the same company as Lauren and me?'

'No, I don't. I used to, once upon a time, but I decided it wasn't for me. Lauren's great at it all, though.'

'Yeah, she really is amazing. She's fierce with contractors, charming with clients and she's really nice to the staff. She's the best boss I could ask for. Well, she sent me here for free – that shows how nice she is! Sorry, I'm rambling. So, what do you?'

He laughs. 'You really don't need to apologise for going on about how great my sister is. It's very sweet. Mia would not speak in the same tone.' That's the first time he's mentioned her name all night – or ever really, apart from introducing us. 'I persuaded my dad to invest in some businesses around here. So we pump money into failing restaurants, bars, hotels. And I'm in charge of turning them around and making the businesses boom again. Eventually, they can buy us back out again if they choose to. It's going well. I think I've found my forte.'

'Wow, sounds exciting!' I say in admiration.

'Yes, it is. Well, I enjoy it anyway. And the place I ordered the pizza from, that's one of the businesses we're invested in, hence it was free.'

'Ah, OK! Well, it is great pizza. You're on to a winner there! And that's why you're staying here then, I take it?'

'Indeed, it is. It really took off about a year ago, so I decided I needed to be here more. You can get more done in person. I'm too easy to ignore at the end of a phone. But I'm afraid I haven't spoken to Lauren for the last eighteen months, so she wasn't to know. I tend to head back to the UK when the family book this place out. Which means I get the best of both worlds.'

I don't know if it's rude to ask or rude to brush over it, so I decide to just go for it and ask him, 'How come you've fallen out? That's such a shame. I mean…you don't have to explain. You can just tell me to butt out if you want!'

He rubs his head. I'm not sure if he's working out *if* he should tell me or *how* he should tell me. 'I'd better not say too much, seeing as you work with her. Let's just say it's Mia related. On that note, I'm going to take myself to bed. Thank you, for a most enjoyable evening.' He stands up and touches my shoulder. 'Goodnight, Amy.'

His touch stirs something deep inside me. 'Goodnight, Alex,' I manage.

CHAPTER TWELVE

The next morning I'm woken to raised voices coming from outside. I go over to the bedroom window and peer out. Alex and Mia are arguing on the driveway. She's throwing her arms in the air and pointing her finger in his face. Moody Mia, I think to myself, I wonder if she ever smiles. She throws some keys at him and storms off down the driveway. Alex starts to turn around, so I quickly throw myself on the floor. I don't think he caught me watching. I go over to Steph's room and gently knock.

'Come in!' she calls.

I go in and climb into her bed. 'Budge over!'

She wriggles over a bit. 'You OK, babe?'

'I'm great. I had a lovely night in. How about you. Did he meet your expectations?'

'Yes, he did, thank you!' she says, stretching out her arms with a huge smile on her face. 'Ah, I'm sorry, Ames. This is supposed to be *your* rebound holiday!'

'It's fine,' I say. 'I'm enjoying the relaxation. It's just what I need. Pool day or beach day?'

'I quite fancy a pool day.'

I get up and throw the sheet over her face. 'Get your ass out of bed, then! We can laze in the sun and catch a tan!'

She laughs and pushes the sheet off her. 'Well, you seem to be in a good mood this morning. Is there anything I'm missing?'

'Nope, nothing to report...' I close her bedroom door and whisper, 'Yet!'

We chill around the pool all day stuffing our faces with cold pizza. I seem to have my appetite back. There's been no sign of Alex. I was thrilled when Steph suggested a pool day; I thought I'd get to see more of him. I told her how we'd hung out last night, what he does for a living and how he doesn't speak to Lauren. But I omit the details about how I much I enjoyed myself, and how it felt when he touched me. I feel different about Alex. It's not a usual crush; I feel this intense connection.

We've decided to have a relaxed evening, have a stroll around the shops and go for a nice meal. I put on a long green dress with white flowers and a pair of flats as we're going to be walking. I make an effort to curl my hair and put on a little bit of make-up, just in case I see Alex at some point this evening.

I decide to text Lauren. I'm supposed to be keeping her updated, but I can hardly tell her I fancy her brother! I message her: *Hi Lauren. Having a lovely time. I'm glad we stayed in the villa. Alex has been very accommodating. Tan is coming along nicely x.*

I go downstairs, grab a bottle of white wine out of the fridge and pour us a glass each.

Steph comes in and asks, 'Still no sign of Alex?'

'Nope,' I reply. 'Do you think he's OK? I did hear him arguing with Mia on the driveway this morning.'

'Did you? What was that all about?' she asks, eager for gossip.

'I don't know. I didn't really hear what they were saying. My windows were closed and I had the air con on. He did give me his number. Do you think I should message him?'

She looks at me surprised. 'When did he give you his number? Did I miss something?'

I take a big gulp of wine. 'No, he just gave me his business card before we went to the beach yesterday. Just in case, you know, because of Shaun.'

'Oh, and then he came to the beach.'

'Yeah?' What's she getting at?

'And then you spend the night together, and there's a big argument with Mia?' she asks inquisitively.

'Hmm-mmm,' I say, trying not to give too much away.

'Yes! Message him, woman! Alex and Mia fall out the night after you pair hit it off. Strike while the iron's hot, babe!'

'OK!' I squeal excitedly. I rummage through my bag and find his card. It reads: *Alex Stevenson, Property Investment & Development Manager*. I put his number into my phone and start typing a message: *Hi Alex, it's Amy. I just wanted to check you're ok. We've not seen you today.*

Steph is leaning over my shoulder. 'Kiss, add a kiss!'

'No way! I'm never going to be the first one to add a kiss again!' I say. Although, I do debate it in my head before sending. I would normally put a kiss just to seem friendly anyway. I decide not to and press send.

'Chicken!' says Steph. She kisses me on the cheek and we both drink our wine in silence waiting for a reply.

My phone beeps a few minutes later. I grab it quickly but am instantly disappointed when I see Lauren's name. 'It's just Lauren,' I tell Steph. 'She's glad we're having a nice time. Come on, let's get out of here.'

We're walking back to the villa; the last stretch up the steep driveway is a struggle. I'm knackered from all the walking and the large meal has made me lethargic. We've had a lovely evening, but it's been slightly overshadowed by the fact that Alex didn't reply. I notice his car isn't on the driveway.

When we get in, Steph goes straight to bed. I make a coffee and sit in the lounge hoping that I might catch Alex. Once my coffee is gone, I give in and go upstairs.

No sooner does it seem that I close my eyes, I'm awoken by my phone beeping. I reach for it on the bedside cabinet. It's Alex, and it's three a.m. How come he's texting me at this hour?

I sit up, rub the sleep from my eyes and open the message: *Hi Amy, I'm sorry if I had you worried. There was a situation. I'll be back in a couple of days x.* He put a kiss! I'm about to tap out a reply but think better of it. I don't want him to think I've been sitting around waiting for his message. I'll reply in the morning, at a normal hour. It takes me forever to go back to sleep – I can't stop thinking about him, and the kiss at the end of his message.

The first thing I think about when I wake up is texting Alex back. I grab my phone and run downstairs where Steph is up and making breakfast. 'He messaged back!' I yell with excitement. 'At three in the morning, he messaged back! And, he put a kiss!'

'Woah woah, calm down! Let me see then, Ames. Pass it here!' I show her the phone. 'A situation,' she reads. 'Wonder what that's all about?'

'No idea, but it means he's not ignoring me, so that's good!'

'Yes, it's great! Go sit outside and message back. I'll bring brekkie over in a sec.'

I sit overlooking the pool and write back: *Sorry to hear that, hope everything's ok. See you soon x.*

Steph brings out toast, croissants, butter and jams with some fresh orange juice. 'Thought we'd go continental today!'

'It looks great. Thanks, hon!'

'How do you fancy going on a boat trip today? I picked up this flyer last night – looks pretty decent. Drinks and lunch are included. They take you out to two different places and let you have a swim in the sea – it's even got a slide on it!'

'Yeah, that looks like fun! I can't believe we're on day five already. We're halfway through our holiday,' I say, making a sad face.

'I know, time flies when you're having fun, babe! And when you're hanging out with someone you have a major crush on,' she says with a wink.

'I know. I've only known him a few days. Well, I don't even know him at all, really. I still don't understand the whole Moody Mia situation. But there's something about him. It feels like more than just a crush, you know? Then sometimes I think I'm being ridiculous because he's so gorgeous. What would he want with me?'

'Amy, you are beautiful. You don't realise how beautiful you are! I think that he, whose name begins with a D who we can't mention, seriously messed you up and knocked your confidence. You're a knockout! And Alex would be lucky to win you over!'

'Thanks, but I think you're just biased! And Mia is bloody gorgeous!'

'I mean it, Ames. You are so much hotter than Moody Mia! I like that name you've given her by the way. Yeah, she looked good, but underneath all that designer clothing and expensive make-up, I don't think she's all that!'

'Thanks, Steph, love ya!' I blow her a kiss.

The boat is huge and it has three decks. We're on the lower deck because we just followed the crowd when we boarded. But we agree we want to sit in the sun once everyone's aboard and we get moving.

'Jackpot!' Steph says, pointing to the beer cooler. 'I'll see if we're allowed to help ourselves!' She comes back with two bottles of beer as the boat starts to move. 'Shall we go up?' she asks.

'Yeah let's,' I say, taking a bottle from her and having a swig. It's so refreshing in this heat. We walk around the middle and come across the ladder steps to go up.

'Shall we just go up top?' she asks.

'Yeah, anywhere with a seat, I guess,' I reply.

She's almost at the top when she just stops. I don't realise until it's too late and my head bounces off her ass.

'What's going on?' I ask her.

'Erm, nothing. Just start going back down so I can back up. There's nowhere to sit up here.'

'OK,' I say as I start stepping back down.

Suddenly, I hear, 'Stephhhh!' and a load of whistling.

'Shit!' says Steph as she quickly moves back down the steps and reaches me.

'Oh my God. It's *them*, isn't it? How could you?'

'I'm *so* sorry, Amy. I didn't know they would be on here! I swear I would never have suggested for us to come on here if I'd known!'

'So you didn't arrange this with Paul?' I ask.

'Of course not, babe! I would never! I haven't even spoken to him since we last met! I told him that was it and I was spending the rest of my time here with you! And he respected that. He hasn't got in touch. We said our goodbyes and that was that.'

'OK, well, let's just find a seat on this deck, shall we? We're stuck on here for a few hours now; I don't want them to spoil it!'

We find a seat on the back of the boat and take our tops off so we can tan in our bikinis. I try to put Shaun being on the same boat to the back of my mind. The sea breeze blows my hair around wildly and I can taste the saltiness of the seawater on my lips. I can't believe that idiot's on here. What are the chances! I replay the evening in my mind. How his mood changed like a flick of a switch. I can just sit here and not interact with him. The boat is plenty big enough for us to be able to avoid each other.

'I'm gonna get us another drink, Ames, OK?'

'As long as there's a toilet on this thing,' I reply.

'Course there's a loo! Back in a sec.'

I'm admiring the breathtaking view of the vast ocean and watching the land slowly shrink into the distance when Shaun appears.

'Can I sit?' he asks awkwardly.

'Steph will be back any minute.' I feel the need to clarify that I'm not alone and will have backup momentarily, even though the boat is heaving. He couldn't do anything to me on here.

'I just want to apologise, Amy.'

'And you need to sit for that?' I scoff.

'I tell you what, I'll do you one better,' he says, getting down on one knee. 'Amy, will you please forgive me?' He's holding his hands in front of him as though praying and looking at me with pleading eyes. He has a stupid smirk on his face, which makes me feel like he's mocking me. He's not taking this seriously at all!

I look up and see all the other guys from his stag group leaning over the top deck staring down at us. 'Is this all a big joke to you?!' I scream at him. I can see Steph walking back towards us taking in what's going on. She looks as furious as I feel. As she walks behind him, she nudges him with her foot so he loses his balance and falls over.

'Weyyy!' the lads all cheer and clap. 'Getting beat up by a *girl*,

Shaun!' one of them shouts, and they all laugh.

Steph bends over him while he's still down and says, 'Go and run back to your friends, you little arsehole! Leave Amy alone!'

He pushes himself up. 'Jeez, I was only trying to say sorry!' He's still saying it in a playful way, as though it's a big show for his pals. He walks away, and I glance up to the top. The only one not laughing is Paul; he actually looks mortified.

Steph hands me my drink, pulls me in for a hug and says, 'You OK, sweet? I'm so sorry I left you!'

'Yeah, I'm fine. Thanks for trying to demean him for me. I'm so glad I never took it any further with him. He's a complete knob!'

'Agreed, complete knob, cheers to that!' We clink bottles and laugh as we take a swig. I'm trying to put on a brave face, I don't want him to see that he's got to me, but on the inside I'm horrified by the whole ordeal. People on the boat are now staring at me because of all the commotion. The sooner this boat ride is over, the better.

We've had our lunch, which was a buffet spread on the lower deck. We went down together as Steph won't leave my side now, and I'm so grateful for that. We even go to the loo together – we both just about manage to squeeze in. It's pretty minging in the toilet, as you'd expect on a boat, I suppose. Stinks of piss and there's what we suspect to be piss all over the toilet seat. But we manage to hover over it. Having both of us in there means you can hold onto the other person's arms to keep you up in the squatting position. There's no soap either. Luckily, Steph's organised with hand sanitiser. We've managed not to bump into them so far. They are staying on the top deck, and we are avoiding it.

The boat comes to a stop at the first place for a dip. 'Are we going in?' I ask Steph.

'Only if you want to, honey?'

'Yeah, let's do it. I'm determined not to let him spoil my fun. Let's just wait and see where they go, and we'll get off the boat on the opposite side.'

'Good thinking.'

We can work out where they're all jumping off due to the raucous sounds. They're diving off near the front, so we make our way to the back of the boat and use the steps. I've learnt the hard way about jumping into water wearing a bikini. There'll be no flashing today! We delicately jump off the steps and swim away from the boat to allow room for others to get down.

We're gently treading water and basking in the sun, when suddenly something pulls me under the water by my ankle. Everything goes quiet apart from the sound of water rushing around my ears, and I feel the water pouring into my mouth and up my nose. I panic. Whatever it is lets go, and I push my way to the surface. Steph is also under at this point and helping to pull me up.

As soon as my head is out of the water, I'm coughing and retching, and Steph is pulling me back towards the boat. Now there are hands all over me pushing and pulling me onto the deck. I am laid down on my side, and I vomit up the seawater that I swallowed, along with my half-digested lunch.

'Amy! Oh my God! Are you OK?' Steph is at my side stroking my head.

I'm still spluttering too much to answer her. The organisers are shouting at the people around us to back off and for those in the sea to return to the boat. We're heading back to shore. Someone with a mop and bucket starts to clean up my sick.

'I'm sorry,' I just about manage to say in between coughing.

'Amy, shh… Come here, babe.' Steph and a member of staff are pulling me up to my feet. They take me down onto the lower deck and wrap a blanket around me. Steph is cuddling me and talking to the man, but I'm sobbing too much to hear what's being said. That was absolutely terrifying.

Steph hands me some napkins and a bottle of water. 'Here, babe, let's clear some of these tears away and you can try and get some water down ya. The nice boatmen are going straight back to shore now to get you checked out, OK? You gave me quite a scare there. Do you know what happened?' I drink some of the water. 'Little sips, honey, OK. We don't want you chucking ya guts up again, do we?' says Steph, trying to make me laugh.

I would laugh at her if I didn't feel so drained. All my energy has been zapped. I try to speak. 'It felt…it felt like a hand… around my ankle…pulled me under!'

'You *think* it was a hand or *know* it was a hand?' she asks, her face deadly serious now.

'It couldn't have…been anything…else. I know it was…a hand.'

'That bastard!' she screams.

'You think…it was…Shaun?' I ask, scared to know the answer but pretty damn sure I already know.

'Yeah, I do. I saw him swimming not far from us when I was pulling you back to the boat. Who else would it bloody be?'

CHAPTER THIRTEEN

Once we get back to shore, we're taken straight off the boat before anyone else and led into a little hut. There's someone waiting for me; I'm unsure if it's a first-aider or a paramedic. She checks me over, listening to my breathing through a stethoscope on my chest and back, and then she checks my pulse and pupil response. While doing all this, she asks a few questions before deeming me fit to leave. After Steph hands me my bag and clothes, I dress myself.

'Has everyone left the boat?' I ask. 'I don't want to see anyone. That was so humiliating.' Steph pops her head out and nods to me. I thank the paramedic and the boat people for being so nice and can't help but apologise again.

'We're just going to sit in this bar while we wait for a taxi, OK? I'm going to get you a cuppa,' says Steph, guiding me into the nearest bar.

'Sure.' I sit down when she pulls a chair out for me. She goes over and speaks to the waiter and when she comes back, I'm sobbing again.

'Aww, Ames, come here!' She wraps her arms around me and holds me tight. 'That bastard isn't going to get away with this, I promise!'

I let her hold me for a while, it's comforting, and it's hiding my tearful face from the passers-by. She only moves when the waiter comes over. He places two cups and saucers, a teapot, a jug of milk and a bowl of sugar on the table.

'Gracias,' says Steph.

I look up and see that she's been crying, too. 'What's the matter, hon?' I ask her.

'I just can't believe he did that. That scared the life out of me back there! And you've done nothing to that evil bastard. All you did was withhold sex, which is your bloody right! And you've come here to get away from knobheads like him, and we're supposed to be having a great time, and it's all my fault because I spoke to them in the first place!' Her tears are coming thick and fast now.

I grab her hand across the table. 'None of this is your fault, Steph. Don't you dare blame yourself! I love you.'

'I love you,' she says and tries to fight back her tears.

I start making her tea, but she slaps my hand away. 'Don't you dare! I'm supposed to be looking after you!' She immediately takes over the tea making.

I take a sip, it tastes so good, filling my mouth with warmth and taking the disgusting taste away. I drink it in no time, and she makes me another.

Suddenly, Alex comes running over to us; he hugs me without saying anything.

I'm stunned. He holds me for what seems like an eternity, and I'm dying to ask all these questions: What is he doing here? How did he know we were here? Why is he hugging me? Does he know what happened? But I'm so satisfied to be in his arms that I just stay silent and accept the hug for as long as I can.

When he eventually pulls back, he holds my face in his hands and asks, 'Are you OK?'

I nod my head; I seem to have lost the ability to speak.

'I hope you don't mind, but I messaged Alex from your phone while you were being checked over,' says Steph. 'I told him what happened and asked him to pick us up.'

I shake my head to indicate that I don't mind.

'Shall we get you home?' asks Alex. I nod my head, and he pulls me up out of the chair. Then he bends down and before I realise what he's doing, I'm in his arms. I put my arms around his neck, rest my head on his shoulder and let him carry me to the car.

I wake up in my room, where Alex carried me when we got back.

I was so exhausted. I think I fell asleep as soon as my head hit the pillow. It looks dark outside. What a traumatic day. I still feel drained in my body, but my mind feels awake. I don't want to be alone after the day I've had. I decide to go downstairs to see if anyone's about.

Alex is sat in the lounge. There's a lamp on and a couple of candles burning. He looks so handsome, the candlelight flickering against his skin. He turns when he hears my footsteps.

'Hey, what are you doing out of bed?'

'I just woke up and didn't feel much like being on my own,' I say.

'Come here and sit. Shall I make you a coffee?'

'Thanks, but I think I'm entitled to something a little stronger, after the day I've had!' I sit next to him.

'Very true. One gin and tonic coming up!' He gets up and goes to the kitchen.

I suddenly realise I've not even checked my reflection before coming down. I bet I look a right state! I try to comb my hair with my fingers the best I can. It's so knotty from all the wind on the boat – I don't stand a chance.

He comes back in with two big gin bowl glasses full to the brim and clinking with ice. 'Here you go, milady!' he says, passing one to me.

'Thanks,' I say, feeling myself blush. *Milady*. Probably just a random comment, but it makes me feel special nonetheless.

He sits down next to me and raises his glass. 'To a shitty day!' and we clink glasses.

'To a shitty day,' I reply. 'So, you kinda rescued me again,' I say, taking a big gulp of gin. Ah, that's good. 'I didn't think you would be back yet,' I add.

'I wasn't going be, but I had to come back and rescue my damsel, didn't I?' he says, smiling at me.

'You didn't have to come back, just for me. I was already rescued by the time you got there, to be fair,' I say jokingly.

'I did have to come back for you though, that's the thing. I was trying to be there for Mia, but as soon as I knew you were in trouble, I had to come back to be here for you.' He looks up from his drink and into my eyes and says, 'I had to know that you were OK.' He looks back to his drink and takes a swig.

I try to keep my cool whilst inside I'm dancing ecstatically because he must care about me. 'Is Mia OK?'

'Huh?'

'Is Mia OK? You just said you were trying to be there for her?'

'She's getting there. Things with Mia are...complicated. You do surprise me. After the day you've had, you're caring enough to ask how Mia is, and you don't even know her. She didn't even say hello to you when you met her... You're just a caring person though, aren't you?'

'I guess I am,' I say.

'Well, it makes a refreshing change, let me tell you! Mia is so manipulative.'

I carry on drinking, not sure what to say.

After a couple of minutes, he says, 'I'm going to kill that Shaun, just to warn you. Steph told me what he did. I know where he's staying.'

'You don't need to do that. He's not worth it.'

'No, but you're worth it!' he says. 'Amy, I mean this in the nicest possible way, but you look like you could do with a long soak in the bath!'

I laugh. 'Yeah, I feel like I do, to be honest!'

'Come on, bring your gin.' He holds his hand out and I take it. He leads me up to my room. 'Why don't you go and brush your hair and grab your things? I'll run the bath for you. Here, I'll take your drink in for you,' and he takes it off me and goes into the bathroom.

I go into my room and try to locate all my toiletries. I can hear the taps running and I frantically brush my hair. Oh, teeth. I really need to brush my teeth after being sick. I grab my toothpaste and toothbrush and go into the bathroom.

He sees me go to the sink. 'I'll give you a minute,' he says, walking out.

I'm brushing my teeth wondering what's going to happen. I

assume he's just coming back to finish running my bath. But I'm quite capable of doing that myself. He's probably just doing it to look after me, to be nice. After cleaning my teeth, I quickly lock the door and use the loo and then unlock it again when I'm done. I don't want him to think I've locked the door because he's not welcome in here. He is totally welcome in here! After a couple of minutes, he knocks.

'Come in,' I call. He enters the room with the candles from the lounge and places them around the bath. Then he checks the temperature of the bath water with his hand before turning off the taps. He goes over to the switch and dims the lights, and then he turns towards me and puts his hands on my shoulders. He just stands there for a few seconds, looking at me. I see his Adam's apple take a big gulp and his muscles clenching in his jaw. I don't feel like I can breathe. His hands fall gently down to my waist. I catch my breath. He stops, examining my face. Then he begins to lift up my top. I raise my arms and he pulls it over my head.

'What about Mia?' I whisper.

'There is no Mia,' he whispers back. Then he hooks his thumbs into my shorts and just stops there and waits, looking at me. Then he kisses my shoulder, and I shudder. As he looks up, I bite my lip playfully. He kisses my shoulder again and gently tugs on my shorts. He then kisses my chest, my stomach, my hip bone, my leg, my ankle, all the way down until my shorts are on the floor. It feels divine! I have never wanted anyone so much in my life as I want this man right now.

He stands back up and gently strokes his fingers around my back, reaching for my bikini string. He places one hand firm on my back and uses the other to yank at the bikini string, untying it. Then he moves up to the string around my neck and does the same. My bikini top falls to the floor and he stands back to look at me. He's tightly pressing his lips together and breathing heavily.

I step forward, put my hands on his back and gently feel his body until I reach the bottom of his T-shirt. I lift it over his head. Oh, that body. I trace my fingers along his pecs, over his nipples and his six-pack until I find his shorts. And I do the same to him. I kiss him on his shoulder, pecs, stomach and hip while I pull down his shorts, over his bulging underwear.

I stand back up, our faces so close, both of us almost naked, and our lips haven't even touched yet. I lean closer to kiss him and when I'm almost there, he pulls back and smiles. When I go to kiss him again, he does it again and a little laugh escapes. He's such a tease! Then, finally, our lips meet, for the softest, most gentle kiss.

My nipples gently rub against his bare chest and everything feels sensational. I find myself groaning. I don't think I've ever groaned just from being kissed before. We break apart reluctantly, and he's searching my eyes again. Inside, I'm screaming, *'You have permission if that's what you're after! Just take me already!'*

Satisfied with whatever my facial expression has told him, he finally removes my bikini bottoms. He stands back admiring me before pulling down his boxers. Now my turn to admire him.

He takes my hand and helps me into the bath, and then follows me in. He sits behind me, hands me my drink and begins to lather me up. I've never had a man wash me before. He does it all very lovingly, and when he's finished rinsing each body part, he kisses it. When I'm clean from top to toe, he turns to face me in the huge tub. He gently lifts my chin to kiss my lips again.

He then gets out of the bath and helps me out. He's about to hand me a towel but shakes his head. 'You look so sexy all wet. Why on earth would we want dry you?' He leans me against the door, pushing us through the doorway into the bedroom. Neither of us can stand the suspense any longer.

The next morning, I wake up feeling completely content, but I'm alone in the bed. I start to panic. What if he didn't enjoy it? What if he was just using me? Oh God. What if I'm a Mia rebound!

I sit up and there's a note by the bed. A piece of paper folded in half with 'Amy' written on it. It's leaning against a cup of coffee. I put my hand to the cup. It's cold. Damn. I unfold the note.

My dearest Amy,

I deeply apologise for abandoning you this morning, I had to run an errand. I assure you, my absence is in no way a reflection of what happened last night. Quite the opposite in fact. I do hope you are willing to partake in a repeat performance.

Yours, Alex xxx.

My heart pounds in my chest and I squirm with excitement under the bed sheet. OMG, I need to tell Steph! I throw on my PJs and run to Steph's room. I don't even knock; I just barge straight in and get into bed with her.

'Morning, Amy! What's going on? How come you're so happy this morning after everything yesterday?' She sits up and studies my massive grin. 'No! You didn't?' I nod enthusiastically. 'Oh, babe, I'm well chuffed for you! Come here!' She hugs me and just as quickly as she pulled me in, she's pushing me away again. 'Come on, then! Spill, damn it! I want every single detail!'

CHAPTER FOURTEEN

I'm relaxing by the pool with not a care in the world and a piña colada in my hand. Even with everything that's happened since we got here, it's turned into the best holiday of my life! Last night made yesterday's ordeal worth it! Imagine if that had never happened yesterday – Alex wouldn't have come back and last night wouldn't have happened! In a weird way, Shaun has done me a favour trying to drown me! Nothing is going to bring me down off this high. I am on cloud nine.

Suddenly, there's a knock at the door. I wonder who it could be.

'I'll get it,' says Steph.

I carry on sipping my piña colada whilst humming the Piña Colada song and soaking up the sun.

Steph comes back out. 'Amy, can you come in a minute? It's the police.'

I sit bolt upright. 'What?'

We walk into the kitchen, and there's a policeman and a policewoman. The policeman, I'm surprised, is English. He looks to be in his late fifties, balding and with a moustache. He asks if I know where Alex is. The policewoman is definitely Spanish. She's got that whole gorgeous Latino vibe about her. Beautiful olive skin and golden brown shiny hair.

'Ahem, do you know where Alex is?' he says again, snapping me out of my trance and bringing me back into the room.

'No, I'm sorry, we don't.'

'Well, when he gets back, you need to get him to call us ASAP, OK? Tell him it's George he *needs* to ring. He knows who I am – he's got my number.'

'OK,' I say. 'May I ask what this is about?'

'He's been spotted near the scene of a crime. We just need him to come and make a statement so we can rule him out, that's all.

Nothing to worry about.'

'It doesn't sound like it's nothing to worry about!' Steph pipes up. 'What sort of crime, exactly? We're staying with this man, and we hardly know him! This is quite alarming to us!' she says, fretfully.

'Well, ordinarily I'd ask why you're putting yourself in a dangerous position shacking up with a bloke you hardly know!' he scoffs. 'But, as I said, I know Alex, so you got lucky this time. You've got nothing to worry about. I know the Stevenson family personally. You're in good hands there. Some young kid has been beaten to a bloody pulp. Anyway, get him to call me ASAP, OK?'

Steph and I both nod our heads silently and wait for the two officers to leave. As the door closes behind them, we look at each other with panic in our eyes. I put my hand to my mouth trying to stifle the scream that wants to come out.

'Try ringing him, now!' shouts Steph. I crouch down on the floor, unable to move with shock. Steph paces around the room. 'Look, we could be jumping to the wrong conclusion here, Amy. It could just be a coincidence,' she adds and then pulls me up from the floor and into a hug.

'It's a bit of a *strange* coincidence that yesterday Alex said he was going to *kill* Shaun for what he did to me, and now the police are trying to find him because someone has been beaten to a bloody pulp! Don't you think?'

'We don't even know if the beaten-up person is *Shaun*, honey!'

'Text Paul!'

'And say what exactly? "Oh, hi, Paul. By any chance, has your mate been beaten to a pulp?"'

'Just text him to say hi and see if he tells you anything? And I'll try ringing Alex.'

'OK,' she agrees reluctantly.

We're walking into the town. I'm going in search of Alex,

and Steph is meeting Paul. He's not mentioned anything about Shaun, so we still don't know if it is him. But he was up for meeting Steph, so we agreed that she should go and then we'll find out either way.

Alex hasn't been answering his phone. My stomach feels like it's tied in knots. Steph told me to be rational and that the nice policeman didn't even think it was him, but the way Alex has been with me, so protective over me, I just keeping thinking the worst. How badly beaten up is he? What if he's actually killed him? He'll go to prison! Worse, he'll go to a foreign prison! You hear horrible stories about how they treat prisoners abroad. I always thought that's how prisoners should be treated, to be fair. We're too soft in the UK – you hear about them sat in their cells with TVs and PlayStations. But now, to think of Alex sat in a foreign cell, refused any privileges and eating gruel. For what? For a justified crime, really, in my opinion. The scumbag deserved it. If it was Shaun. It could all just be a misunderstanding. I need to keep calm.

'Amy!' Steph shouts.

I turn around. She has stopped on the pavement and she's holding her side. 'What is it?' I shout back and start to walk over to her.

'Just a stitch. I'm trying to keep up with your power walking – you're like bloody Wonder Woman or something!' she replies, panting.

'Sorry,' I say, and realise that I'm panting myself. I've been so focused on finding Alex. Steph passes me a bottle of water. I take a few sips and hand it back. 'Ready now?' I ask.

'Ready,' she says and goes back to half walking, half running alongside me.

'I found it!' I turn and say to her. 'The pizza place is over there, up that side road – look!'

'Oh yeah! Well, good luck, hon. And remember, don't go in there all guns blazing. We don't know all the facts. You can't go accusing Alex of a crime we don't know he's committed. If it is all a misunderstanding and you go ranting and raving at him over nothing, you'll look like a fool. And any chances of "repeat performances" will be out the window. OK?' she says, holding my shoulders, trying to maintain my eye contact, which keeps wandering over towards the pizza restaurant. It's definitely the right place; I recognise the logo from the pizza boxes. It's called Prego. It's the only place I know to try and look for him. 'OK? Promise me?' asks Steph.

'Promise. Good luck with Paul.' We hug, give each other a kiss on the cheek and go our separate ways.

As I approach the restaurant, I slow my pace and scan the tables looking for his familiar face. I don't see him. I decide to go in, order a drink and hang around in case he appears. He mentioned investing in a few businesses. He might not even be there. Chances are slim.

I choose a table in the middle and sit with my back against the wall so I can see both directions. I'm directly opposite the bar and the door that leads to the kitchen. I keep watch hoping to see his face pop up.

The restaurant interior is typical. Red and white checked tablecloths with white plastic disposable covers over the top to protect them and held down with metal clips. All restaurants abroad seem to do this. You wouldn't ever come across it in England. I wonder, with all the concerns over the damage caused to the planet by plastic, if this ritual might be phased out eventually. The chairs are white plastic; I can feel my bum starting to stick to it with sweat already – nice!

The waiter comes over to take my order, and I notice it's the same guy who delivered the pizzas the other night. 'Hola! Are you ready to order?' he asks, flipping the pages in his notebook to find the next clean page.

'Can I just get a drink please?' I ask in my most polite tone.

'Si, of course, of course.' He places the notebook back in his pocket.

'Just a Fanta Limón, please.'

'Fanta Limón,' he repeats and walks over to the bar.

When he reappears with my drink, I thank him and then ask,

'Is Alex here today?'

He looks at me for a second, then clicks his fingers and points. 'Oh! From Alex's house! The pizza order!'

'Yes, that's me!' I declare.

'Ah! Alex did come this morning, but no longer here, I'm sorry.'

'Do you have any idea where he might be? Only, he's not answering his phone,' I say, waving my phone in the air as if he can't understand my English and I need to demonstrate what I mean, when clearly he speaks pretty good English.

'Er…he mentioned going to Hotel Azul.'

'Do you know where that is?' I ask, hopeful.

'Si, it's about a ten-minute walk, on the main strip, next to Bar Loco.'

'Brilliant, thanks so much for your help!'

'*De nada!*' he says, walking away.

I drink as much Fanta as I can because I am actually really thirsty, but it's too gassy to finish. I saw Hotel Azul when we were in the bar. It's the hotel where the stag do lads are staying. I leave a ten-euro note on the table under the condiment tray holding the oil, vinegar and salt so it doesn't blow away. Then I unstick my behind from the chair, and I'm grateful to feel a breeze.

'Gracias,' I call out to the nice pizza man, who I feel like I could kiss right now, as I leave the restaurant.

He gives me a wave and goes straight to the table to pick up the money.

I'm just walking around the corner of the bar; the hotel is down a side street on the opposite side of the road. I'm not sure what I'm going to do when I get there. I walk through the revolving door and the feel of the cool air-conditioned reception area is bliss. I can hear Alex's charming voice. He's here! I see him sitting in the lobby with two other men. They look like they're talking business, so I hang back. I walk over to the noticeboard and peruse the various posters while I wait, every now and then stealing a quick glance in their direction.

After what feels like forever, but it's probably about twenty minutes, he spots me. 'Amy?'

I turn around. 'Oh hi!' I reply, forcing myself to act casual and breezy.

'What are you doing here? Is everything OK?'

'Well, I do need to talk to you about something – something important.'

'Sure, shall we sit down?'

'Yeah, sure.'

He leads me to the table where he was sat previously and pulls his phone out of his pocket. 'Oh, I have rather a lot of missed calls from you!'

'Yeah, I've been trying to reach you.'

'I can see that! And how did you track me down to here, Miss Marple?' He smiles.

My heart melts. 'The police are looking for you. Someone called George. He wants you to call him right away.'

His expression changes to one of concern. '*OK...* Any idea what about?'

How do I word this without him thinking I'm being accusatory? 'He said there was a man, who had been beaten up, and that you need to give a statement.' There, stick to the facts I know.

'Oh yeah, that was outside here earlier. When I first arrived early this morning, there was an ambulance and a couple of police cars. I heard them saying they'd found someone down the alleyway pretty badly beaten up. I watched for a bit before I came in here for my meeting. That's probably when they spotted me.'

'And you've been sat in here the whole time and they didn't find you?'

'Well, not exactly. We've been in a meeting room. I've only been out here the last half an hour. I'd better call George and see what he needs from me. I'll be right back, OK?'

'OK.' He walks away to make his phone call. My phone rings, it's Steph.

'Hi!' she manages to say.

I can hear her crying. 'Steph, are you OK?'

'I'm fine. Look, it *was* Shaun that was beaten up.'

I look over at Alex; he seems so calm and collected. I watch him on the phone smiling and chatting away as if nothing has happened.

'Amy!'

'Sorry. So it was Shaun, is he OK?' I ask, even though I'm not sure that I actually care about his condition.

'Amy, it was Paul.'

'What?'

'It was Paul, who beat up Shaun. I could tell from the moment I met up with him. I'm sorry I didn't call earlier. He was just in such a state. He was so upset. His hands were all bloody and swollen.'

I look straight at Alex's hands and see that they're perfectly intact – those perfect, gentle, manly hands. It wasn't him... I feel such relief that I start to cry. 'Why did Paul do it? Are you OK?'

'I'm just a bit emotional, sorry. It was tough to see him like that. And he's about to hand himself in. I tried to talk him out of it. But he said it's the right thing to do. Shaun was bragging about what he did to you and taking the piss out of you. And he said he just lost it! He said he didn't really know him that well; he'd only met him a couple of times before the stag and had never really liked him. He was one of the other guy's mates. But they all just watched Paul lay into him for a while before they pulled him off. They all knew he deserved a pasting, but Paul was the only one with the balls to stand up to him. When they dragged him off, they told him to leg it.'

'Oh my God! Where are you now?'

'I'm just at Charlie's bar. We're having one last drink together before he goes to the police station.'

'I'm with Alex now. We'll be right there, OK. Don't tell him we're coming and scare him off, though!'

'OK, babe, thanks.'

Alex walks back over with concern all over his face. He sits next to me. 'What's the matter, Amy?' he asks, rubbing his big thumbs under my eyes, removing my tears.

'The person who was beat up, it was Shaun.'

'Was it indeed? Well, that is bloody karma for you, isn't it! I have to say, that has made me ecstatic! Why is it making you upset? You don't still have feelings for him, do you?' He looks disappointed.

'No, of course not! I was crying because I was relieved! When the police came asking, I thought…we thought…maybe you had done it.'

He's laughing now and hugs me with his big arms and kisses the top of my head. He holds my face and gently plants a soft kiss onto my lips. 'As much as I would like to have been the person to do it, I'm afraid someone got there before me.'

'Well, the person who did it was Paul, the guy that Steph's been seeing.'

'Wasn't he supposed to be his friend?'

'He was on the same stag do; he didn't really know him that well. And he beat him up because of me. Because of what he did to me. Steph's with him now, but he's about to go and hand himself in. I really don't think he should volunteer himself. I feel partly responsible. I mean, he's got what he deserves, hasn't he? Do you think he could get away with it? Is that wrong of me to want him to dodge the law?'

He runs his fingers through his hair as if contemplating what I've just said. Eventually, he looks at me. 'Usually, yes. I wouldn't agree with "dodging the law", as you put it!' he says with a laugh, but within a second his face is serious again. 'Where are they? Let's see if we can talk him out of it.'

I throw my arms around him and give him a big squeeze. 'Thank you! They're at Charlie's bar.'

'We'd best get going, then.'

◆ ◆ ◆

We get to Charlie's bar and find Steph and Paul hidden away at a corner table. Steph is still teary, and Paul doesn't look great either. His eyes are all red and he looks worn out. I run and hug Steph, then I hug Paul. He looks a bit surprised. Alex holds his hand out to Paul and waits for him to shake it. He seems reluctant to, but after a couple of seconds he raises his hand from under the table and shakes Alex's outstretched hand. I can see why he was hesitant. His knuckles look terrible. Alex keeps hold of his hand and inspects it.

'Have you put any ice on this, mate?' he asks him.

'Nah, haven't had chance. Didn't want anyone to see, and ain't been able to go back to my hotel.' He quickly puts his hand back under the table.

Alex gestures for me to sit and then goes over to the bar.

I sit next to Steph and look at Paul. 'Thank you. He was a nasty piece of work and he deserved what you did to him! And I really don't think you should hand yourself in.'

'But I have to, dun I?' He shrugs. 'I dunno how I can get away with it.'

Alex comes back with a tray of four G & Ts and a glass full of ice, a tea towel draping over his arm like a waiter. He places a G & T in front of each of us. When he passes mine, he says, 'Milady,' and winks. He sits next to Paul, takes the towel off his arm and tips the glass of ice into it. He wraps it up and hands it to Paul under the table.

'Cheers, mate,' says Paul.

'It's me that needs to thank you, Paul. You saved me a job, to be honest. And I will do everything in my power to protect you. So, we're going to enjoy our drinks, and then we're going to go back to mine, OK? You've done the right thing by keeping a low profile. Can you trust everyone else from the group you were with?'

'Yeah, I think so,' he replies.

'Well, you need to know, so drink up. You've earnt it.'

We arrive at the villa at around nine p.m. We've drunk quite a bit of gin and we're all a bit wobbly. We wanted to wait until it was dark so nobody noticed Paul or his hands. Alex has said that he can stay here while we try to figure things out. Steph is overjoyed.

Once they've gone to bed, we're in the lounge cuddled up on the sofa together. I'm lying in between his legs with my head resting on his chest, my arm around his waist. Just being in this close proximity is driving me wild inside.

'Thank you for everything you're doing for Paul,' I say to him.

'That's OK,' he replies, stroking my head. This is all so new, and yet it feels so comfortable and easy. 'He really has done me a favour. It would have been me facing prison otherwise if I'd caught him.'

'You wouldn't have really, would you?' I ask.

'I think I just might have. And it scares the hell out of me, to be truthful. I'm not usually an angry person, but I would absolutely do that after what he did to you. When I heard what had happened, I was filled with rage. You're so sweet, gentle and nice. I can't believe how he's treated you.'

As much as I'm enjoying the comfort hug, I need more. I want more. I turn myself around and pull myself up so I'm lying on top of him, face to face. I lie holding my upper body slightly above him on my forearms. I can feel myself trembling slightly, and I can feel his breath against me. It's like electric. We're hardly touching and there's all this energy bouncing between us. I lean down and tenderly kiss his lips, wanting desperately to kiss him harder, but withholding. Eventually, when we can no longer stand it, we kiss deeper, and I press my body hard against his.

He gently sits us both up and peels my dress over my head. I pull off his shirt and my hands are all over his body, pulling him against me. The feel of his skin against mine feels incredible. We squirm around each other removing the remainder of our clothes, our lips never parting other than to pant for breath. I take him inside me, and my world is blown away.

CHAPTER FIFTEEN

The next morning, I awake in Alex's bed, with Alex lying next to me. My feet do a little happy dance beneath the sheets. It feels surreal. I'm also very aware that it's day eight. I feel a pit in the bottom of my stomach. I'm so not ready to leave this man; things have just started to get good. Great, in fact. All my fidgeting makes him stir. Without even opening his eyes, his lips find mine. It doesn't take long before he slides me beneath him, and I wantonly pull him to me.

We all gather around the dining table for breakfast. Alex has cooked a Spanish omelette, which we're tucking into with toast. We all have slightly sore heads, so we're stuffing our faces in silence. I can't stop looking at Alex, and I feel myself grinning like a little schoolgirl every time we make eye contact. I would be embarrassed if he didn't have the same stupid look on his face.

'Oh my God, you two are *so* cute!' says Steph, eyeing us both.

I shyly look away after being caught and try to concentrate on eating.

Paul's hands are looking better, the swelling has vastly reduced, but they still look sore. 'I'm supposed to be goin' home today,' he announces. 'Am I gonna be OK to go home? I'm still not sure I'm doin' the right thing.'

'You're doing the right thing, Paul. We're not going over this again,' says Steph, stroking his shaven head.

'I'm going to make some enquiries, see what I can find out,' Alex says and leaves the room, eyes glued to his phone, thumb scrolling over the screen.

'You should go and have a bath, Paul. The bath here is amazing! And it'll make you feel so much better,' I say to him.

'A bath?' He looks unconvinced.

'It's big enough for Steph to join you,' I offer.

'Oh, well, in that case...' he looks at Steph, and she beams at him.

'Come on then, race ya!' she says, pushing herself up and running towards the stairs.

'She is barmy,' he says to me. 'D'ya know that? Bloody barmy!' and he runs after her.

I clear away the dishes and fill the sink with hot soapy water. I don't hear Alex sneak up on me over the sound of the water, and he makes me jump when he snakes his hands around my waist and plants a soft kiss on my neck.

'What did you manage to find out?' I ask him.

'I found out quite a lot, actually. Shaun is awake, and he told the police he was mugged, by a local. So, Paul can go home – as long as he keeps his hands hidden and doesn't raise any suspicion.'

'That's fantastic news!'

'Yes, it is. Where have they gone? I was going to share the news with them,' he says, scanning the kitchen and looking for them through the patio doors.

'For a bath,' I say. 'I thought Paul could use one... You might wanna give them a minute,' I add, raising my eyebrows.

'Oh, I see! That makes things even more perfect, then. Now I have time to ravish you.' And with that, he lifts me onto the kitchen island.

We're lazing around the swimming pool. Steph has gone to see Paul off at the airport. It turns out he only lives about forty-five minutes away from Damsbury, so they've agreed to see each other again in a couple of weeks. Now that I've built up my tan, I'm wearing my white bikini. Alex has been on the phone a lot, work calls. He paces around the pool area talking away, but he keeps looking over at me, and I know now that when he gives me that intense look, it means he wants me. I pretend not to notice and carry on reading my book. I think it's driving him crazy. He can't see through my oversized sunglasses that I'm constantly glancing over to him, checking him out. I giggle to myself. I don't think I've ever had so much sex in such a short space of time. I just can't get enough of this man. I'm so not ready to go home.

My phone beeps. It's Lauren: *Hi, just checking in to see how it's going! Hope you're still having a good time! X.*

Oh man, I forgot about Lauren. How am I supposed to tell her about me and Alex? I'm not even sure myself what me and Alex are. I know he makes me feel amazing, not just in a sexual way. He makes me feel different, like no one else has before. I don't ever want it to end. He may feel differently. I don't think he does; it feels like we're both on the same page. But who knows, maybe I'm reading too much into it. Maybe to him this is just a fling. I'll be gone in a couple of days. He could just be thinking it's a bit of fun.

I text back: *Hi Lauren. I'm having the BEST time! Don't want to come home. Thank you again! xx.* There. I'm not lying. I'm just not filling her in on all the information as to why I'm having the time of my life!

A new message comes back straight away: *Are you now! Sounds like you have gossip? I thought you were going to keep me updated! xx.*

Damn, caught out. I reply: *Fill you in soon, promise! xx.*

Alex is now lying on the lounger next to me. 'Do you know how hot you look right now?' he says. 'You are awfully distracting!'

'Am I? Well, I'm sorry to distract you from your work,' I reply, acting coy. 'I'm going to take my *hot* body for a dip in the pool to cool down.' I strut over to the pool and slide in with all the grace I can muster. I force myself not to react to the cold water that's making me want to scream, trying to act cool. I roll onto my back and glide through the water. After which, Alex jumps straight in after me.

We're in the villa making a cocktail when Steph gets back. 'Hiya! Ooh cocktails! That was good timing! What are we having?' she asks whilst taking a seat at the kitchen island.

I retrieve a third glass from the cupboard. 'We're attempting to make strawberry daiquiris. Here, see what you think,' I say, filling her glass.

'Mmm, that is delicious!'

'Is it really?' I ask and fill the other two glasses. I take a sip. 'Yep, that's pretty damn good,' I agree.

'I hope it's worth all the mess you created!' Alex says, tapping me on the bum. He takes a sip. 'Yeah, OK, it was worth it!' he agrees. 'Did Paul get off OK?' he asks Steph.

'Yeah fine. I was actually quite sad to see him go. I can't believe our holiday is coming to an end, babe,' she says to me.

'Don't remind me,' I say as I feel a wrenching in my gut.

'Steph, would you mind terribly if I stole Amy from you tonight for a romantic meal?' Alex asks.

My spirits lift slightly. Aw, that would be so nice. I look at Steph, and she has a strange, shocked look on her face.

'I'll take that as a no, then? I'm sorry – it was rude of me to ask.'

But she's waving her hands and shaking her head. 'Brain freeze! Brain freeze! Sorry, too much frozen daiquiri! Of course I don't mind! Amy didn't mind when I went out for a night with Paul. Why would I mind? On one condition, though! You make me a big batch of strawberry daiquiris to keep me company tonight!'

I laugh. 'Done! Aw, thank you, Steph! You're the best!' and I give her a huge hug. 'So, taking me somewhere romantic, are you?' I ask Alex, intrigued.

'Yes, I am. Thank you, Stephanie. You had better go and get yourself ready then, Amy,' he says.

'Come on, Ames! I'm gonna help you get glammed up! It's time to wear *the dress*, babe!'

'Ooh, the flowy one you bought me?' I ask her.

'That's the one! Let's go! Bring the daiquiris!' she orders.

Steph is amazing at glamming me up. I've showered, every-where is freshly shaven, and Steph has made sure every inch of my body has been moisturised with this glowing moisturiser of hers. It's amazing, with a slight gold shimmer to it. She always has the best stuff. She's meticulously blow-dried my hair and curled it. She's used about four different products, which I must make a note of because they've made my hair look fabulous. She's backcombed to add volume in the all the right places and semi-brushed out the curls to give me the most lustrous, mag-nificent wavy hair. I've never been able to get my hair to look this good. She's now applying my make-up; I feel like she's been at it forever. I swear she's used about twenty different brushes on my face. I don't understand what half of them or the pallets she's using actually do – it looks completely confusing to me.

'Ta-dah!' she says, announcing that she's finished.

I look in the mirror. Wow! 'How did you do that? How did you get me to look like that? That's insane!'

'I'm glad you likey!' she says with a boastful smile.

'I likey a lot,' I say, checking my reflection from every angle. My eyes really stand out with how she's applied my eyeshadow and eyeliner, and the mascara she's used makes my lashes look three times their natural volume and length. My complexion looks absolutely flawless and bronzed to perfection. And my lips are super shiny, but not at all tacky. This stuff is amazing. I've never had a lip gloss that isn't tacky – when the moment the wind blows, half my hair sticks to my lips.

'Have you finished checking yourself out, hot stuff?' asks Steph. 'Because it's time to get dressed!'

I'm wearing my sexiest lacy underwear – matching for a change, too. She holds the dress above my head and slides it over me. Then she pulls out a pair of her shoes, gold strappy sandals with high heels.

'I'm not sure I'll be able to walk in those!' I remark.

'You will! And they will make your legs look bloody gor-geous, trust me!'

'OK,' I say apprehensively.

She straps my feet in and places a thin gold chain around my neck, which has a pendant that sits perfectly in my cleavage. 'Perfect,' she says and steps back admiring her handiwork. 'Amy, you look so bloody stunning, babe. Absolute knockout!'

I check out my reflection. This has to be the best I've ever looked. 'Steph, will you please be my personal styler and get me ready every day?' I ask.

'You couldn't afford me, babe! Sorry! Now, get your sexy ass down those stairs and make his jaw drop to the floor!' she says with a wink.

'You're the best. Thanks, Steph. Love ya!' I go to kiss her, but she pulls away.

'Uh-uh! No wrecking the masterpiece!' I roll my eyes. 'Oh here, take the lip gloss with you – be sure to keep those lips topped up! Oh! Your perfume!' She sprays me a few times. 'There, now go!'

'Thanks, honey!' I make my way down the stairs being sure to hold onto the rail, petrified that I might stack it at any moment in these shoes. Alex is in the kitchen whizzing up some more daiquiris for Steph – bless him. When the noise of the blender stops, and he hears me walking into the kitchen, he turns around. Oh. My. God. I thought this man could not look any sexier, but here he is in a full-blown suit. Is he not going to be hot in that? Well, I can always help him take it off. I realise he is gawking at me too.

He takes a step towards me and runs a hand through his soft hair, his other hand on his hip, drinking me in. 'Amy...you look incredible!'

'Thanks.' I blush. 'You don't scrub up too bad yourself!' I say cheekily.

He walks slowly towards me, exhaling as he goes. When he finally reaches me, he plants a soft, gentle kiss on my lips, one hand holding my cheek, the other hand on my back. 'And you have your perfume on that drives me insane!' he whispers into my ear, nuzzling at my neck. My body begins to writhe in reaction to the feel of his lips on my skin.

'Ahem! Sorry to interrupt, but carry on like that and you pair will never make it to the bloody restaurant!' says Steph.

Alex begrudgingly pulls away, and we both giggle like teenagers caught snogging. 'Apologies, Steph – and yes, you have a very good point. Although, I have to say, I can't say I'm hungry much any more...for food anyway!' he says.

I tap him on the bum with my clutch bag and bite my lip.

'Yes, well, some of us aren't getting any tonight, so maybe you could just behave until you're out of my presence, eh? You're making a lonely girl feel jealous over here!' says Steph.

'Your daiquiris are all whizzed up and ready to go,' Alex says, and I see that he's blushing.

'Aw, thank you, hon! Now, both of you, get outta here – and, Ames, gloss!' she says, pointing at her lips.

Oh, he must have kissed it all away. I reapply it as we walk through the door and get into the waiting taxi.

The restaurant is on the seafront and it's beautiful – a completely different experience from the pizza restaurant. It looks very upmarket and modern. No tacky plastic tablecloths here. They're thick white cotton and pristine. No plastic chairs either; instead, they're solid wood with black leather. Candles are lit on each table.

The waiter seats us on the terrace overlooking the beach, and I can hear the waves crashing against the rocks. Alex speaks to him in Spanish, and he returns with a bottle of expensive-looking champagne and two glasses.

Inside, I do a little happy dance. This is just perfect. Champagne is the perfect drink to go with this setting. I'd never have been treated to anything like this with Danny. The only place he'd really take me to was The Bull, and he'd never entertain drinking anything that wasn't a pint of bloody lager.

Once the glasses are poured, Alex takes a sip and nods his approval. He leaves the bottle in the champagne bucket and we're handed two menus. I've never understood this taste the wine malarkey. My mum always said it was to check the wine wasn't corked, but I've never actually seen anyone take a sip and then refuse the wine.

He hands me a glass. Even the glass is fancy, I notice. He points his towards me and says, 'To a wonderful evening.'

'Cheers,' I reply and chime our glasses together. Hmm, must be crystal, I think to myself before taking a sip. Mmm, it's so bubbly and delicious. I open the menu and notice everything is terribly expensive.

'What do you like the look of?' he asks whilst eyeing the menu.

'Besides you?' I ask, chewing the inside of my cheek.

He lets out a slow, sexy laugh as he looks at me and rubs his chin. 'You're making it very difficult for us to get through this meal as it is, just sitting there looking irresistible. Keep making flirtatious comments like that, and I'll be ripping that dress off you before the entree arrives!' I giggle.

The meal was divine. I'm quite thankful there wasn't much of it; I didn't want to feel bloated and lethargic, not tonight. We went through a bottle and half of champagne, and I'm feeling very giggly and giddy. The waiter comes over with the bill, and Alex immediately picks it up and ushers away my offer of paying towards it. A true gent.

'Thank you, the meal was exquisite. And this place is done out so tastefully. It really is beautiful.'

'Yes, it's my favourite restaurant here.'

'Are there any more like this?' I ask curiously.

'There are quite a few restaurants that produce delicious food, but none are furnished quite as nice this one.'

'I know pizza isn't fancy, and would never be seen on the menu here, but that pizza you ordered me from Prego was delicious. Yet, I bet they lose out on business because the restaurant itself is so off-putting. It's a shame.'

'Really? It's off-putting?' he asks, intrigued.

'Yeah, well, I'm no expert – obviously, that's your department! But they could make that place look less tacky and more inviting, and I bet they'd attract a load more custom.'

'A load more custom?' he ponders, amused.

'Well, OK, it's probably not the professional way of putting it,' I say, suddenly feeling like a fool for even bringing it up. This man is an expert in turning failing businesses around, after all. I should have kept my thoughts to myself.

'So, just out of interest, what would you change about Prego?' he asks, placing his elbow on the table and cupping his chin with his hand.

'Well, it wouldn't need to be as fancy as this place obviously, but I'd chuck out those plastic table covers for a start.'

'I have already recommended they should be replaced with paper versions – more economically friendly.'

'Oh, well, I wouldn't bother. I'd chuck out the red and white checked tablecloths too. And replace all the furniture... I'd replace the plastic tables and chairs for wood or something. White tablecloths. Remove all condiments from the middle of the table and replace with centrepieces. The whole place needs a lick of paint and all the posters removed from the walls. I mean, I get that they're advertising other local businesses and I assume they advertise theirs in return, but you don't need them plastered all over the walls – leaflets can be left on the bar or given out with the bill. Then it needs some good lighting, fresh flowers on the bar, a couple of nice pictures on the walls, and it would look like a completely different place! They'd get away with bumping up the price of the pizza to cover the makeover, I'm sure.'

He sits back and folds his arms whilst looking at me. He's chewing his cheek and narrowing his eyes.

'What?' I ask.

'Not just a pretty face, are you?' he says. I blush at the compliment, although I'm not sure if he's mocking me.

I go to the loo and quickly freshen up. When I return, he stands, picks up the bottle with the remaining champagne and holds his hand out to me. I take it and we walk out of the restaurant towards the beach.

He sits me on the step and unfastens my shoes, kissing my foot and leg as he does so. 'These are very sexy indeed,' he says. He passes them to me to hold, picks up the bottle, and we hold hands and step onto the sand.

The feel of the cold sand beneath my feet is wonderful. And my feet so are glad to be out of those shoes for a bit and walking flat again.

He takes a swig of champagne and passes it to me; I take a swig. 'Just as I first found you, look – swigging from a bottle!' He laughs.

I nearly spit out the bubbles with a snort but try my best to hold it in. When the laughter subsides, I'm finally able to swallow. 'Yeah, I forgot about that! It seems so long ago now, yet it was only a few days ago. Weird.'

'From that moment I first saw you, dancing half naked in my swimming pool, swigging wine by the bottle, I knew...'

'Knew what?'

'That I had to have you,' he says, kissing my hand.

I really want to mention the fact that I'm going home in two days, but I can't bring myself to spoil this perfect evening. We carry on walking down the beach hand in hand, taking turns with the bottle, not saying a word, not needing to.

'Do you mind if I get a selfie of us?' I ask, realising I have no photos of him at all.

'Yeah, sure.'

'Great!' I pull my phone out. We try to get the sea in the background, but you can hardly see it because it's so dark. The sea breeze is blowing my hair all over the place and we're both laughing as we have to keep retaking it. Finally, I get the perfect shot. You can see our hair blowing, we both look extremely happy, and neither of us have our eyes closed. 'Thanks,' I say.

'Can you send me that, please?'

'Yeah, of course.' I'm chuffed to bits that he wants to remember me too.

When we get back, it's dark and quiet. Steph must be in bed. The moment we're through the front door, he pushes me against the wall and delicately kisses me all over my neck, shoulders and chest.

'I cannot resist you for a moment longer! It's taken all my strength not to do this all night!' he says between kisses. Every kiss sends a jolt through my body. 'Come,' he says, standing and leading me to the stairs. 'Ladies first,' he says.

I do my sexiest strut in heels up the stairs slowly, and he follows behind. I turn to see him biting his fist and staring at my ass.

'I think you need to leave those shoes on!' he says.

I giggle and walk as fast as I can to his room.

CHAPTER SIXTEEN

I wake up the next morning with Alex still asleep next to me. I have mixed emotions. I'm so happy being with Alex, but I know I have to go home tomorrow. My dream has to come to an end. My head is telling me it's a holiday romance and that I should have known from the start. But my heart says I don't want to go; this man has entered my life and made me feel so different. I'm not leaving the same person as when I came here.

After gliding my hand across his stomach, he is instantly awake. He turns facing me and pulls me into the longest embrace.

'I have to go home tomorrow,' I whisper.

'Do you absolutely have to?' he whispers back.

'Would you want me to stay?' I ask.

'Yes,' he answers without hesitation.

'Really?' I ask, surprised.

He releases me and looks straight into my eyes. 'I would love you to stay, Amy.'

I feel overjoyed that he actually he wants me to, but in reality it's just not practical. 'I wish I could,' I say.

'Well, why can't you?'

'Erm, because I have a job to go back to, and my normal life?'

'Your job is with my sister. I'm sure I could sort things out there.'

'Even though you don't speak to her?'

'I'm pretty sure I could sort it out, if you wanted me to. Is there anything you would want or need to go home for, other than your job?' he asks.

I think about it for a minute before replying, 'No, I suppose there's not really.'

'No house?'

'No, I still live with my mum and dad,' I say, embarrassed.

'Then, I guess the question you need to ask yourself is would you rather stay here with me or go back to your job?' he asks with a nervous look on his face.

'Without a shadow of a doubt!' I beam. 'Although, I would feel guilty for leaving Lauren... And you would actually want me to give everything up, and stay here, with you?' I ask.

'Without a shadow of a doubt,' he replies.

I'm smiling the biggest smile. Yet, I feel a little scared. Am I really going to give up my job and everything for a man I've just met? But most of all I feel over the moon that he wants me to stay. And I'm sure that wherever he is, is where I want to be. I know it's not rational. Anyway, my mum and dad will probably go crazy. It's not the sensible thing to do. I think Steph will even be pissed at me.

He rolls me over. 'So, does that mean you're staying?' he asks while kissing my bare back and heading further under the covers with each kiss.

'Well...I have to...speak to...Steph.' I struggle to get my words out as I'm distracted by his lips. 'But...maybe,' I say in between moans of pleasure.

'Well, let's see what we can do to turn that maybe into a definite.' He then disappears beneath the covers.

I go into Steph's room and climb into bed with her.

'You OK, beaut?' she asks.

'I'm great, thanks. You OK? Was your night OK last night?'

'Well, it was fine until you guys got home and all I could hear was you pair having what I assume was the best sex of your life!'

I hide my head under the sheet. 'Oh sorry, were we loud?'

'Don't be sorry, babe, I'm only jealous! You guys seem so into each other. Like smitten! Two little smitten kittens!'

'He's asked me to stay,' I say, steeling myself for a lecture.

'You're shitting me!' she says a bit too loudly, and I have to shush her.

'It's a ridiculous idea, isn't it? I should just go home. I'm not Shirley bloody Valentine.'

'Hell, frigging no!' she roars. 'What's waiting for you at home? I'm sorry, but rich, super-hot, blatantly amazing-in-bed man asks you to stay in an awesome villa with him in the sun. Or... you can go back home to rain and your boring low-paying job and live with your mum and dad – no offence to Sue and Jim. Oh, and there will be zero sex, and zero hot men... Do I need to go on? I mean, it's a bloody no-brainer, honey!'

'You reckon?' I'm surprised. I honestly thought she'd be dead against it and bring me back to reality. I can't believe she thinks I should stay too.

'What's the worst that could happen if things don't work out? You go back home and find a new job. If you go home now, you'll be kicking yourself wondering what could have been if you'd stayed!'

'True. Thanks, Steph. You're the best,' I say, snuggling up to her.

'I know, hon, I know,' she says, patting my head.

Steph and I are out shopping. Now the holiday is coming to an end, she's buying all the things she's been eyeing up all week.

'Black or silver?' she asks, holding up two pairs of sandals.

'I think silver,' I say.

'Oh, I wanted the black.'

'Well, why ask my opinion, then?' I shrug with irritation.

'D'ya know what...I'm just gonna get both – they're only fifteen euros each!'

I let out an exasperated sigh. We've been shopping for about two hours now and because I'm not buying anything for myself, I'm reaching my level of boredom. 'Drink time?' I ask.

'Always! Just let me go pay for these, babe.'

I walk out of the shop and wait for her outside. It's strange to think I won't be going home with her. I'm so nervous about it all. My head is screaming, "What are you doing, you muppet? This isn't normal – you've known him for five minutes!"

But my heart is telling me that I need to stay and be with him. And, of course, my libido is all for staying. I've been tearing myself apart inside wondering if I'm doing the right thing. But like Steph says, worst case scenario, I come home in a couple of months heartbroken and I have to find a new job.

Steph appears and breaks my inner argument with myself. We find a nice little bar where it's happy hour. Two-for-one cocktails. Perfect. We both have a Long Island iced tea, because we both know that's the cocktail with the most alcohol.

Once we're on our second, I unlock my phone and start a message to Mum. 'What am I gonna say to her?' I ask Steph.

'Met hot rich man, not coming home?' she suggests. I laugh so loud that people turn to look. 'OK, how about, fell in love with hot rich man, not coming home?'

'I'm not sure I'm in love! It's a bit early days for that,' I say.

'You're not fooling anyone here, Ames. You have the love bug. As does Alex. It may be too early days to admit it, but it's written all over your smug little faces!'

I smile and start my message to Mum: *Won't be back home tomorrow. Going to stay a bit longer, having such a great time. Call you soon xxx.* I show it to Steph before sending.

'You know she's going to call you as soon as you send that?'

'Shit.'

'Yes, shit. You need to have all your answers read for Mama Sue. She's going to want to know everything!'

'Maybe I should wait. I don't even know the answers myself yet.'

When we get back to the villa with Steph's ten shopping bags, Alex appears at the door. 'You've been busy, ladies!' he says, taking the bags off us to carry them through. Ever the gent.

'Steph's been busy, not me. I don't have the cash to splash like this one!' I say, rolling my eyes.

'I'm exhausted. I'm just going for a siesta. Give you guys a bit of alone time.' Steph winks and makes Alex blush.

'Been dragging you around all the shops, has she?' he whispers.

'Yes,' I whisper back and stick out my bottom lip.

'You know I would've given you money to buy something if you'd said?'

'I wouldn't take your money!' I say defensively. 'I can earn my own, you know. I don't want you to think I'm with you for your money, because it's certainly not your money I'm interested in!'

'I didn't say that. Look, go and get your sexy bikini on, Miss Independent! Business meeting, in the swimming pool, in ten minutes. OK? You look like you could use a dip.'

'Is that a nice way of saying I'm a big sweaty mess?'

'Yes, that was the polite way,' he says, kissing my sweaty face.

I run up and change into my bikini as requested. Did he say business meeting? Ready. I pile all my hair on top of my head and put on my shades. When I get downstairs, he's waiting by the edge of the pool.

When he sees me, he takes his T-shirt off and throws it onto a sunlounger. I will never tire of looking at that muscly torso. I walk over and wrap my arms around him, my cheek against his chest.

He pushes me back a step, his jaw clenched. 'Let's just keep a certain distance between us so I can restrain myself – just until the business discussion is done. Come.' He jumps into the pool.

It makes me so happy to know that I drive him as wild as he drives me. I jump in after him.

He pulls two inflatables over that I haven't seen before. One is a unicorn ring, and the other is a chocolate doughnut with sprinkles. He drags them over to the steps. 'A unicorn for you. I want you to be comfortable while we discuss business,' he says.

'I love it!' I say, surprisingly planting my bum in the ring successfully on the first attempt.

He climbs into his doughnut ring and paddles his arms in the water to catch up with me.

'So, what's this business meeting all about, then?' I ask.

'Well, if you have decided for definite that you're going to stay, then I have a proposal.'

'An indecent one?' I ask with a pretend shocked face.

'Well, the proposal I hope is decent, but we have plenty of indecent things we can do later.'

I giggle and try my best to swirl back so I'm facing him, as my unicorn takes on a mind of its own and floats in the opposite direction. Suddenly, I'm gliding backwards; he's pulling my unicorn by the tail back over to him.

'You said earlier that you didn't want my money – but clearly, you're going to need some money. And if you refuse to take mine, you need to earn some.'

'Yeah, I thought about getting a job in a bar or something.'

'I think I can do better for you than that. Besides, I don't want you strutting around in Bar Loco in a bikini giving out shots. I'd have to be there protecting you from all the lecherous men!'

'Ha! That wasn't quite the job I was thinking of, but I like that you think I'm hot enough to be one of those shot ladies!'

'You are hotter than those ladies, trust me. But what I'm proposing is that you work for me.'

'Work for you? But I don't know the first thing about what you do?'

'On the contrary, you do, you pitched it to me last night.' I look at him puzzled. 'Prego. You can renovate Prego.'

'Really? You'd put me in charge of that?'

'Yes, obviously I'd help you with the various suppliers and contacts. But you will be in charge of all the decisions. Within a budget I set.'

'That sounds awesome! But how do you know if I'll be any good at it? Aren't you taking a bit of a gamble?'

'Well, I thought your idea was great. I've managed to make cost reductions with suppliers, and we've bought new kitchen equipment and computerised tills. But you're absolutely right. It needs a fresh look. Something to attract the clientele away from the neighbouring restaurants. And, you've been working for Lauren for how many years?'

'Erm…seven. My God, seven years!'

'So this shows me that one, you are loyal; and two, you must be good at something when you put your mind to it, because you still work there. For Lauren. The pickiest person when it comes to staff traits.'

'How come she pays me so little money, then? If you reckon she thinks I'm so good?'

'Because it's business. Have you ever asked her for more money?'

'No, I wouldn't dare!'

'Well then, it's a case of "If you don't ask, you don't get". If you were to say you'd found a job elsewhere, I bet she'd have offered you a salary increase as an incentive.'

'Like now, you mean?'

'Not exactly. I hope you wouldn't go running back home if she offered you more money to stay there?' he asks, looking slightly wounded.

'Of course I wouldn't!' I splash water onto him, and he splashes me back. 'I want to stay here, because you're here. And I can't bear the thought of not being with you,' I say.

He pulls my unicorn towards him so we're side by side and kisses me. 'I hoped you would say that. So, do you like the sound of the job?'

'I love it! Thank you. And now I can give my mum a reason to stay that she won't think is stupid and naïve!'

'You're welcome. I look forward to us working together.'

'Will all of our business meetings be in the swimming pool?' I ask, clapping my hands.

'Well, some might be in the bedroom...perks of sleeping with the boss! Talking of which...shall we go and get showered?'

'Absolutely!'

CHAPTER SEVENTEEN

Alex is cooking us a barbeque tonight for Steph's last night. I still can't believe it's not going to be my last night. It's super scary, but in a good way. I still haven't broken the news to Mum and Dad, or Lauren. It's bite the bullet time shortly. I'm now helping Steph pack her things.

'Why does it never fit in the case on the way back?' she says, rejigging her suitcase for the third time.

'Maybe because you're also trying to cram in everything you bought earlier!'

'Yeah, there is that!'

'Oh, your shoes I borrowed. I'll go get them from Alex's room.'

'Babe, you can keep 'em. You look great in them – and let's not forget, you told me what you did in them! I think it's safe to say they're yours now!'

'Ha, thanks, hon. Alex will be pleased!'

'I'm sure he will.'

'Are you sure I'm doing the right thing?'

'For the tenth time, one hundred per cent. You've gotta take chances in life, beaut! And Alex is a real catch. You're not gonna find one like him again.'

'Thanks. I'd better go down and call Mum and Lauren.'

'Good luck, hon!'

First, it's time for Alex to call Lauren. I think I'm dreading this call the most. Although she won't be my boss any more, she has always been so good to me. She sent me on this holiday, and she's going to find out that I've slept with her brother!

'It's ringing,' Alex announces. 'Hi, Lauren... I know, it has been a long time... I'm sorry... No, nothing has happened to her... Well, actually, I am ringing about her...only she's thinking of staying...staying here... With me, yeah... Yes, as in like *that*... I know, it's been a bit crazy. I'm sorry we didn't really have time to tell you. Would you mind if she didn't come back to fill her position? Would it leave you in the crap? No, OK, that's good... No, it is not my intention to mess her about... Yes, I know she's amazing...I think so, too.' After spending all this time listening to a one-sided conversation, he turns to me and says, 'She wants to speak to you.' Oh crap!

I take the phone from him. 'Hi, Lauren,' I say nervously.

'Hi, Amy! So that's what you meant by you're having the *best* time? You've shacked up with my brother?'

'Erm...yeah...I mean... I'm sorry, I didn't know *then* that I was staying. It was only decided today.'

'OK, and you really like each other, yeah? Like, might be *love* going on here?'

'Maybe.'

'And Mia is out of the picture?'

'Yeah. Well, apparently. I bloody hope so!'

'OK, put him back on.'

I hand the phone back. 'She wants you again.'

'Hi... Yes...yes definitely... This time for good... OK...that sounds great... Thanks, sis. Oh, and it really was great to speak to you... Bye.' He hangs up.

'So?' I ask, wide-eyed.

'So, she said yes. You can stay. She will even keep your job open for three weeks, just in case you change your mind.'

'Wow! That's brilliant! Thank you!'

'Thank Lauren,' he says. 'Not thinking of running back so soon though, are you?'

'Not at all! But it just gives me peace of mind, you know. This is all very new, and things always seem good when they're new, don't they? Of course, I hope this is different. It feels different, right?'

'A simple *no* would have sufficed,' he says, grinning. 'Your turn then, Amy!' Oh crap. Time to call Mum and Dad.

I down half my glass of wine and then hit the dial button. 'Hi, Mum.'

'Hi, Amy love. How are you? Are you having a nice time? Are

you looking forward to coming home tomorrow?'

'Erm, I'm great thanks. I'm having the best time, and that's kind of what I'm calling about...to answer your questions in order.'

'Oh no, has your flight been delayed? That's awful. They're so unreliable these airlines these days with all their strikes!'

'No, Mum. That's not what I'm saying. I've met someone, and he's asked me to stay, and he's offered me a job here.'

'What? So you're not coming home, and you have a job there, and a new *boyfriend*?'

'Pretty much, yeah. Were you just relaying the message for Dad?'

'Yes, sorry, darling, he's sat next to me. It all seems very sudden, don't you think? What's he like? How do you know he's not a nutter? Do you have a job contract?'

'He's amazing, Mum, he's not a nutter because he's my boss Lauren's brother, and no job contract yet. But it's his business I'll be working for.'

'And what does Steph think of it all?'

'Steph encouraged me to stay.'

'Well, she's got her head screwed on, that girl. Is he there? Can I speak to him?'

I hold the phone out. 'She wants to speak to you.'

'Don't worry, I'm good with mums,' he whispers, taking the phone. 'Hi, Mrs Dixon... Sue... My name is Alex Stevenson... I sound handsome and posh? Yes, I did repeat that for your daughter's benefit, sorry... Yes, she's going to stay here in the villa... Job is ready to go...and my sister will keep her old job open for three weeks, in case she decides to come home...because I think she is incredible... Oh OK... Hi, Mr Dixon...Jim, sorry... Yes, that's right... I will look after her, don't you worry... You know, you're both more than welcome to fly out here and stay for a week if it'd make you feel better?'

I yank the phone out of his hand. 'Hi, Dad!'

'Hi, sweetheart! So, we can come and stay, eh? Free digs?'

'Yeah, sure. Well, maybe a bit later on. Let me see if I enjoy it and get settled first, yeah?'

'Sure, love. Well, I think he sounds great. We look forward to meeting him, don't we, Sue?'

I hear Mum in the background say, 'Ooh yes, can't wait. When are we going?'

'So, I've got to go now, Dad. Say bye to Mum. Love you both, and I'll ring in a couple of days, OK.'

'OK. Bye, Amy, we love you.'

'Bye, Dad.' I hang up and look at Alex. 'You invited my mum and dad over?'

'I didn't mean immediately, but they've obviously got concerns about this. If they came and met me, and saw the villa, and you working, maybe they'll understand and approve?'

'You're bloody awesome, do you know that?' I give him a big squeeze. 'That all went better than expected didn't it?' I say with relief.

'Yes, it did. Barbecue time?'

'Yep, barbecue time. You're not some nut job that's going to do me in the moment Steph leaves, are you?'

'No, I promise you I'm not. But then again, if I was "some nut job", I would hardly admit it now, would I?'

'Hmm…very true. I guess I'm just going to have to trust you!'

'I know it's only been a few days, and we hardly know each other, and everyone probably thinks we are crazy, but intimately, I'd say we know each other very well. And that connection we have is not something I am ready to give up.' As he strokes the side of my face, I have to catch my breath.

'Me neither,' I reply.

Alex has set the patio table; it looks fantastic. We have wine, breads and oil, olives, salad, cured meats and dips. And he's cooking a selection of meats on the barbecue whilst I catch up with Steph on our phone calls home. We are now stuffing our faces with olives and washing them down with wine.

'See, it's all working out so perfectly!' says Steph. 'And Lauren keeping your job open for three weeks, that's so generous!'

'I know, she's so good, isn't she? Do you think she thinks it's bound to fail in that time and that's why she said it?'

'No, not at all! She's doing it to be supportive to you I think. And to give you the confidence to try this out, knowing you've got a safety net to fall back on.'

'True. On the phone to Lauren, he said yes definitely, this time for good. What do you think that was about?'

Alex is standing behind me with a platter of barbequed meat and places it in the middle of the table. 'Instead of wondering, you could just ask me,' he says. Crap.

'Sorry, I wasn't talking behind your back. I was just replaying the conversation and trying to figure out the words I missed!'

'That's OK. Help yourselves.' He gestures to the meat. 'She asked if I'd definitely broken up with Mia. I said yes definitely. She asked if it was for good this time. I said yes, for good.'

'Oh, sorry. I feel like I'm prying on a private conversation now. I thought it was about us,' I say, wishing I'd never opened my big gob.

'Technically, babe, it is about you, though? She was checking Mia's out of the picture to make way for you. So, I think you have a right to know that. Doesn't she, Alex?' says Steph.

'Indeed, she does,' he agrees.

'See, nothing to be worried about. Alex is a perfectly normal gentleman. Not a psycho like he who shan't be named whose name begins with D, who probably would have gone batshit crazy if you'd asked him something like that!'

'Hmm... He who shan't be named whose name begins with D?' asks Alex, smirking.

'Let's not go there tonight! Let's just enjoy our last evening with Steph and get pissed. But not *too* pissed that she's hanging out of her arse on the plane tomorrow!'

'I'll drink to that!' shouts Steph.

'To Steph not getting *too* smashed,' Alex cheers. 'Although, it would have been a perfect ending to see you both completely wasted dancing in the pool again, like at the start of your holiday! What a shame!'

'The night is young, Alex, the night is young. I might just get that pissed yet. I wouldn't write it off!' Steph says with a giggle. Oh, I'm going to miss her!

I guess I should have known it was never going to be a quiet night with Steph the party animal. Even when she's got a flight the next day, there's just no stopping her! She's got the tunes on, we're dancing around the patio having a great time and we're all having such a laugh.

Alex can really dance...this man just seems too perfect! Beyoncé's 'Crazy in Love' is playing, which is my and Steph's cue to get up and shake our asses like she does in the video and see who can do it faster. Alex sits to watch and drinks his wine while laughing at us and clapping.

'C'mon then, Alex? Who wins?' shouts Steph.

'You both shake your asses very much like Beyoncé, but if you're going to make me pick one, you know I'm going to choose Amy's!'

'Fair enough! I'm going to get another bottle!' says Steph, bumbling her way into the kitchen.

I walk over to Alex and straddle him in the chair, taking his face in my hands and kissing him deeply. He puts his hands on my bum and pulls me closer.

'Guys! Come on this is my *last* night! You have plenty of time for behaving like that when I'm gone!'

I jump off Alex's lap. 'Sorry, Steph!'

'I'm only jealous!' she says. 'But punishment for making me jealous is getting in that pool! Come on, it's pool party time!' And with that, she strips down to her underwear and jumps into the pool. I turn around to Alex, he's shaking his head laughing, and I start taking my dress off.

'You two are absolutely crazy!' he says.

'Yeah, but you love us!' shouts Steph.

I start to walk slowly backwards towards the pool, beckoning him to follow. He stands up and removes his T-shirt and runs towards me grinning. I turn around and jump in before he can reach me. As I sink to the bottom of the pool, I see him jump in next to me. I pull myself towards the surface and as Alex's head appears out of the water, he swims over to me. He grabs me by the waist and lifts me above his head just like in *Dirty Dancing*.

Steph is whooping and singing 'I've Had the Time of My Life', and then we lose balance and I crash into the water.

He's immediately lifting my head above the water. 'Oh my God, sorry. I really didn't mean to chuck you in like that!'

'It's fine!' I laugh, rubbing my eyes gently to not disturb my waterproof mascara.

Steph is out of the pool and fiddling with the music. 'Alex, you legend! We are *so* listening to the *Dirty Dancing* soundtrack now!'

Alex lifts me and puts me into the floating unicorn, and Steph leans over handing me a glass of wine. As I bob about in my unicorn sipping my wine, I watch the pair of them and realise how lucky I am. I have the most awesome best friend a girl could ask for, and now I also have the most amazing boyfriend. A thought occurs to me. We haven't actually declared that we are an official couple. Alex swims over to me and holds onto my unicorn.

'I don't mean to sound twelve, but are we...like...officially boyfriend and girlfriend now?' I ask.

'I suppose we haven't made it official,' he says. 'Amy Dixon, will you be my girlfriend?'

'Yes!' I squeal, and he pulls himself up to kiss me, but his weight just tips the unicorn over. I completely lose all the wine, but I manage to save the glass. Steph cheers and we all crack up laughing.

CHAPTER EIGHTEEN

I wake up the next morning feeling like death. My head is pounding and my mouth is so dry. I need water. I look at the clock. It's ten o'clock. Steph doesn't need to be at the airport until four p.m. It's a good job she didn't have a morning flight; we'd never have bloody made it!

I wonder where Alex is. I drag myself out of bed and throw on my PJs. I think about knocking on Steph's door but decide to leave her to sleep it off a bit. I walk downstairs and I can hear Alex talking. He must be on the phone; the conversation sounds a bit heated.

As soon as he sees me walk into the kitchen, he says, 'I've got to go,' and ends the call. He looks a bit flustered.

'Everything OK, Alex?'

'Yes fine, it's just work. How are you? How's your head?'

'Urgh! I feel horrid! I don't suppose you have any paracetamol and a gallon of water?'

'Of course. I was down here a couple of hours ago for the exact same thing! I can't remember the last time I drank that much; you pair are a bad influence!' He opens a cupboard and pulls down a box full of medicines.

'Well, it's really Steph that's the party animal. But yeah, if you get the pair of us together and add alcohol, we do tend to go a bit crazy! It was fun though, wasn't it?'

'I haven't had that much fun in a long time. Well, in a *let your hair down kind of way*... Obviously the kind of fun we have together greatly exceeds—'

I stop him mid-sentence with a kiss on the lips. 'You're doing a me now – rambling – when there really is no need for an explanation.' I laugh. 'I'm so glad you enjoyed yourself. My ex would never go out dancing and drinking with me and Steph. Now that I think about it, he was so boring! I don't know what I ever saw in him!'

He places two paracetamol and a glass of water in front of me. I take them straight away and down all of the water. 'He who shan't be named that begins with a D?' he asks, placing a jug of iced water next to me.

'Yeah, him. Let's just say he did me a huge favour! I didn't realise how much I had changed myself to please him. I feel like I'm me again now. The old Amy. Mission accomplished.' I pour myself another water and down it, then I take an ice cube and rub it over my poor head.

Alex laughs. 'You're really dying today, aren't you?'

'Yes,' I say with a pout.

'Well, I have two hangover cures. You can either let me cook you a proper English breakfast—'

'Ooh that one, I choose that one, I'm starving!'

'*Or* we can go upstairs and work up an appetite?' He gives me that look which says he wants to rip my clothes off.

'Ooh no, I choose that one! Hangover sex, definitely!'

He laughs and walks around the kitchen island and takes my hand. 'I'm glad you chose that one.' He leads me up the stairs, into his bedroom and straight into his en suite, turning on the shower.

After I wriggle out of my clothes, he picks me up and puts me in the shower. 'You're always manhandling me!' I say with a laugh. 'Not that I'm complaining,' I add quickly. And he climbs in to join me.

Steph comes down just as we're plating up breakfast. 'Oh, you guys are awesome! This is just what I need!'

I hand her a glass of orange juice, which she drinks all in one go. 'Another?' I ask.

'Yes please, babe.'

Alex puts the plates on the dining table. We've got bacon, sausage, eggs, toast, beans, and he's even done grilled half tomatoes. This is going to make me feel so much better. I put another juice in front of Steph and sit next to her.

'Aw, still choosing me? I thought you'd have sat next to lover boy today!' says Steph.

'Course I'm sitting by you – it's your last day!' We both stick out our bottom lips.

'This is delicious, Alex, thank you,' Steph says with a mouthful of sausage.

'How do you know I didn't cook it?' I ask.

'There's no way you'd have bothered with all of this – especially the grilled tomatoes!'

'You know me so well!' I laugh.

'Got myself a lazy cook, have I?' Alex asks, smiling.

'Oh sorry, I didn't realise you were hiring me as a cook!' I tease.

'Lucky for you, I enjoy cooking, and I'm pretty good at it,' Alex says.

'Alex,' starts Steph, 'I really need a list of your weaknesses, cos at the moment you seem too much like Mr Perfect, and quite frankly it's making me jealous.'

He laughs. 'Let me see… I'm not very good at DIY. I'm no good with fixing cars. I'm generally too trusting of people. I can't sing to save my life. Oh, and I have a maid who does my washing and ironing. So, I'd probably be useless at those too.'

'Well, me and Ames can't sing either…and you'd never have to worry about the other stuff because you're rich enough to pay people to do it for you!'

'Steph!' I say, embarrassed.

'That's OK,' says Alex. 'She's right, I guess.'

'I didn't mean to be rude, sorry!' Steph then looks at me and mouths, 'Sorry.'

'Not at all, I don't think you're being rude. I had a really great time last night, by the way. You pair are absolutely crazy, and I love it!'

'Why thank you,' says Steph.

'And you're welcome back any time, Steph. I mean it.'

'Aw thanks, babe! I'll defo be back!'

'But maybe not too soon. I don't think my liver could handle it!' He laughs.

'So, you only go back to the UK when your family book this place out?' I ask.

'Yeah, but only because I have no reason to really. If you wanted to pop back for a bit, you know you can any time. And I could come with you if you wanted, or not. Whatever you want.'

'How come your dad has an office in Damsbury?' asks Steph.

'Lauren's husband is from there. She was always commuting back and forth from just outside London…and when the old man was ready to branch out and get another office, Damsbury seemed the perfect location. They weren't married at the time. But they had been engaged since she was nineteen. She's always been very focused and driven – knows what she wants and does her best to get it. Have you ever met Richard?' he asks me.

I shake my head. 'She's mentioned him a few times, obvs, but she's never brought him to a Christmas do, but partners have never really been invited. I assumed he was just a boyfriend though, as she still goes by the name Stevenson?'

'No, she's just a modern woman and wanted to keep the name. I assume she wants clients and contractors to know it's her name on the business.'

'Makes sense,' I say, putting down my cutlery.

'I'm going to get showered,' announces Steph. 'I feel minging. I'm sure I smell like I have wine in my hair!'

'You probably have!' I laugh.

We've driven Steph to the airport. As we get out of the car, I start crying my eyes out.

'What's the matter?' asks Alex.

'It's just emotional, that's all!'

'Come here, ya daft cow,' says Steph, even though she has a

couple of tears, too.

'I'm scared of being left on my own without you,' I whisper into her ear.

'You have Alex, babe. You'll be fine.'

'I'll just go and pay for the parking and give you two a minute,' says Alex.

Steph says, 'See, he's such a gent, he even knows when to piss off for a bit!' I laugh. 'I mean it though, honey. I'm at the end of the phone if you need me. And Alex has got your back. He wouldn't let anything happen to you. Look how protective he was over that dick, Shaun. He scared him off in the bar. He was straight by your side taking care of you after the twat tried to drown you in the sea. And if Paul hadn't got there first, I think he'd have done the exact same thing to Shaun.'

'I know. He does look out for me and I do feel safe with him. It's just scary, staying in a new country, with someone I've only known for ten days!'

'I know, but you're totally doing the right thing.'

Alex walks back over. 'Ready, ladies? I think we have time for a quick drink before we usher Steph off to check in her bag and go through security, so you can prolong your goodbyes,' he says, taking Steph's case from her.

'Hair of the dog. I think I might just love you myself, Alex,' says Steph. 'Are you sure you don't want to share him?' she asks me.

'Ha, there's a lot of things I'll share with you, honey, But no, he's all mine!' I say, taking his hand and linking my other arm with Steph's.

We manage to find somewhere to sit whilst Alex goes off in search of booze. She's checking through her bag that she's got her boarding pass and passport, and then she pulls out a little bag and hands it to me.

'What's this?' I ask, taking it from her.

'Open and see!' she says, smiling.

Inside the bag there's a box. I open it to reveal a silver bracelet. It's a thin bangle with a knot in it.

'It's a friendship knot bangle,' she explains.

'It's beautiful, Steph. I love it, thank you!' I give her a big hug.

'Something to remember me by if you start feeling lonely. I notice you didn't bring your nan's bracelet with you. So now you're not going home, I thought you could do with another sentimental piece of jewellery to keep with you.'

'That's so thoughtful, Steph.'

Alex comes back brandishing two miniature bottles of rosé wine and a coffee. 'What's happened in the five minutes I've been gone for you both to be crying again?' he asks.

'Look! Steph bought me this – it's a friendship bracelet,' I say, waving it in his face.

'Ah, that's beautiful. I love how close you two are. Sooo... these are happy tears now?'

'Yes! Now pass the wine! What's with the coffee? Not man enough?' Steph asks playfully.

'Driving,' he explains whilst handing us our bottles and plastic cups.

'Fair enough,' she says, 'very sensible, and yet another reason he's a keeper!' She nudges me. I laugh as we pour our wine.

'I take it you girls don't usually drink this much and it's simply because you're on holiday having a blowout?' he asks.

'Well, I personally have a blowout every Friday and Saturday. Ames doesn't usually drink as much, unless she's with me and I'm corrupting her!' She giggles. 'She's not very good with shots that one. Don't let her at the shots unless you wanna be holding her hair back while she pukes!'

'Steph! *Ten days!* I've known him ten days! You seriously can't be bringing puke up into the conversation!' I cover my face, mortified.

'It's fine. You don't mind, do ya, Alex?'

'Of course I don't mind; it's just a bodily function. And as long as I don't let you have shots, it's a function I'll never have to deal with!' He laughs.

'See, best friend advice one-oh-one,' says Steph, necking the last of her wine. 'On that note, beaut, I think it's time I shoot and join that queue that seems to be growing.'

We both pull sad faces at each other. When Alex clocks us, he pulls one as well.

'Aw, Alex, you're becoming one of the gang. I'm gonna miss ya. Thanks for sweeping Amy off her feet and treating her the way she deserves! It's been a long time coming. And if she tells me that you did anything to upset her, I'll be straight on a plane back here ready to kick your ass! So, you just carry on treating her like a princess, OK?'

I roll my eyes, but I'm so grateful to have a friend like her.

'I would never treat her any less. Stephanie, it's been a pleasure,' says Alex, pulling her in for a hug and a kiss on the cheek.

She hugs him and feels his arms while they're around her. 'My God, they're solid. Have you felt these things? Stupid question, course you have! Come, gimme some love,' she says to me.

We have a cuddle and a kiss on each cheek. 'Safe journey back, hon. I love you, thanks for everything. You're the best. And thanks for my gorgeous bracelet!'

'You're welcome, babe. Thanks so much for a great holiday. I really hope things here all work out for you, and hopefully I'll be back visiting again soon!'

After watching her join the queue, we walk out back to the car holding hands. 'You're really going to miss her, aren't you?' he asks.

'Don't, I'll start blubbering again!' He opens the passenger door and helps me into the car. I'm sure I'll be fine. I might not have a Steph, but I have an Alex.

CHAPTER NINETEEN

Instead of going back to the villa, Alex parks up near the beach. 'If ever I'm feeling shitty, I like to come to the beach. The sound of the waves, the sand between your toes, looking out at the sea. I don't know why, but it's really calming,' he says.

'I completely agree,' I say.

'I thought you might need a bit of beach after saying goodbye to Steph. I know it must be hard for you. I've asked you to give up everything you know, and I know that's a big ask, but I want to show you that taking a chance with me is worth it.'

'Thank you. The beach is a great idea; it's very thoughtful. I wouldn't still be here if I didn't think you were worth taking a chance on.'

He leans over and kisses me, and for a moment I wonder if we'll ever make it out of the car. But eventually he pulls away, plants one more peck on the lips while stroking my cheek, then he's out of the car. I'm a bit disheartened; I was really enjoying that kiss. I remind myself we're in a public place.

Alex opens my car door and takes me by the hand. We stroll hand in hand down the beach along the shoreline, shoes in our hands, and the sun is getting lower in the sky.

'It looks so pretty when the sun is setting,' I say to him.

'It does, doesn't it? Let's go over there,' he says, pointing to a little wooden beach bar hut with plastic tables and chairs outside. He pulls out a chair for me facing the sunset and places one next to me before going up to the bar.

When he comes back, he's holding two ice creams. He hands me one and sits next to me. 'Thanks,' I say.

A couple of minutes later, two cocktails are placed in front of us. They have all the cocktail paraphernalia: umbrellas, concertina paper flamingos, and a big wedge of pineapple with a cocktail cherry that I just love.

'Wow, they look amazing! Thank you.' I dive straight for my cherry before even taking a sip. He hands me his cherry. 'Thanks!' I say, scoffing it straight away. 'Do you not like the cherries?' I ask. 'I don't understand how anyone cannot like those!'

'I do like them, but I like you more,' he says.

I smile and take a sip of my cocktail – it is delicious.

We sit eating our ice creams, sipping our cocktails, watching the sun set. It's so romantic. I feel like I'm falling in love with him. Every now and then, we glance at each other and smile. I feel a bit easier about Steph being gone now. Alex was right; I needed to come to the beach. Looking out to sea seems to take all your worries away.

When we get back to the villa, I'm exhausted. Not that I've done much today, but last night is taking its toll on me.

'What do you want to do tonight?' he asks as I flick off my flip-flops and throw myself on the sofa.

'Erm, pretty much this, all night! I'm still hanging from last night! You don't mind just chilling, do you?'

'Absolutely not, you read my mind! Shall I order us a Chinese?'

'You, Alex, are the perfect man for me! Yes, Chinese! Shall we watch a movie?'

'Yes, film sounds good. What film would you like to watch?'

'You tell me what sort you like,' I say, and in my head I'm thinking please no sci-fi, please no bloody sci-fi. The hours of my life I must have wasted watching crap sci-fi films with Danny – I don't think I could bear any more.

'Well, I like all sorts – comedies, action, bit of horror, drama. I'll even watch the odd chick flick, but don't tell my sister!'

'Do you like sci-fi at all?'

'Erm, not really, but I don't mind giving it a go, if that's what you're into?'

'God no! I'm so glad you said no! Now you just might be perfect!' He leans over to kiss me, and I grab his shoulders and pull him on top of me. His phone starts ringing. Damn.

'Sorry, I'd better just get that as I've skived most of today!' he says, pushing himself up and taking his phone call in the hall.

I get up from the sofa and scan the vast DVD collection in the cabinet. Well, he's not lying; I don't find one sci-fi movie. When I'm hungover, I like to watch something that's not too taxing on the mind. I look for something easy going, which I can watch without really concentrating too much, but will also look pretty cool so he doesn't think I'm a loser. I find *The Wolf of Wall Street* – bloody love that film. I take it out and place it on the floor in front of the TV.

Deciding that I need another cocktail, I go to the kitchen to see what ingredients are left. I notice Alex by the front door. When he sees me go into the kitchen, he walks out of the door signalling 'one minute' to me. I wonder why he feels the need to go through the front door to take a work call. Maybe he thinks I'm going to use the blender for daiquiris and he doesn't want the noise. Fair enough. Ooh, daiquiris, good shout. I go to the fridge and find a large punnet of strawberries. Result! I find the rum and start chucking strawberries into the blender. Hang on, I've been with Alex all day, where did this fresh fruit appear from? He walks back in apologising and looking flustered.

'Everything OK?' I ask, glugging rum into the blender.

'Yeah, well, it will be. I have a meeting the day after tomorrow, and then it should all be sorted.'

'Oh, OK. So where did all these strawberries come from? And everything else that wasn't here this morning?'

'Ah, that'll be the housekeeper, Camila.'

'Wow, I knew there was a cleaner making up the beds and that, but she gets your shopping in too? That's awesome!' I say in amazement.

'Yes, it's pretty awesome,' he replies with a smile. 'Even after a crappy phone call, you just instantly lift my mood. Seeing your happy little face because someone bought strawberries, it's so endearing.'

'Well…strawberries equal daiquiris!' I say.

'Of course, it's awesome!' He laughs. 'No going on a bender again though, hey. Not that I'm telling you what to do, at all. I'm not like that! It's just…well…I have a surprise booked in for you tomorrow.'

'Ooh! What is it?' I ask excited and jumping up and down as I press the whizz button on the blender.

'If I told you that, it wouldn't be a surprise, would it?' he shouts over the blender. He walks into the lounge and reappears in the kitchen once I've poured our glasses and I'm putting the jug into the fridge. He's waving the DVD I chose.

'No good?' I ask, slightly gutted.

'It's bloody perfect. You, Amy, are bloody perfect. This is my favourite film.' He picks me up and puts me on the kitchen island. He starts kissing my ankles, working his way up my legs, slowly placing soft pecks all the way up. As he reaches the top of my thigh, he's suddenly in front of my face and kissing my lips. 'Hold that thought, I'll order the Chinese, then we'll continue where we left off.'

The Chinese was so good. I can't believe how much food he ordered. We had a complete banquet. We were dipping spring rolls in curry sauce, spare ribs, curry and fried rice, beef in black bean sauce, prawn crackers… It was just what I needed for my hangover.

I would never have eaten that much in front of Danny. He'd have been making digs at my weight, calling me a porker. Alex was hand feeding me in between mouthfuls of what I was shovelling in myself. Oh no…maybe he's a feeder and he's trying to fatten me up. No, Mia wasn't fat; I'm sure he's not. I think he's just being normal. I'm just not used to normal. I'm glad we had sex beforehand, because there is no way I can move now. There's about twenty minutes of the film left and I'm yawning my head off.

He pauses it and looks at me. 'Come on, you, time for sleep.' Once he picks me up, I protest saying that I'm fine to walk, but he's having none of it and carries me anyway. He places me onto the bed, strokes my hair out of my eyes and kisses me once before pulling back and staring into my eyes again.

'What?' I ask.

'I... Nothing... Sweet dreams, beautiful.'

'Night, Alex.' I close my eyes and drift off into a long-awaited sleep.

CHAPTER TWENTY

The next morning I'm awoken by him kissing my face all over, then a peck on the lips, head, cheek, other cheek, chin, and he repeats. I arouse giggling. 'Not that I'm complaining, but is there a reason you're waking me up? Ooh, do I start work today?' I sit bolt upright, eyes still closed, and accidently headbutt him. I clutch my head and he clutches his nose. 'Oh my God! I'm so sorry! I didn't realise you were right in front of my face! Are you OK?'

'I'm OK!' he says, rubbing his nose. 'No, you're not going to work today. Well, you can, if you want, but that's not the surprise I have lined up for you. Now, get some clothes on, swimwear underneath, plenty of sun cream, maybe a hat. I'm going to make us a picnic.'

'Ooh, picnic! I love picnics!' I clap my hands like a three-year-old.

He laughs at me. 'You are just too cute. Meet me downstairs in half an hour.' He kisses my forehead. 'You have a red mark on your head. Do you need a cold compress?'

'I'm fine! Sorry again about that!'

'Don't worry. See you in a bit.'

Twenty minutes later, I'm downstairs and see that it's Camila making the picnic, not Alex.

'Hola!' she shouts.

'Hola!' I say back, and she hands me a bacon and egg sandwich. 'Gracias!' I say before taking it and going to sit on the patio, because I feel awkward watching her work while sitting on my arse. I've always been the same. If I'm on holiday and the cleaner comes in, I sit on the balcony. I don't know why, but I feel rude being there and getting under her feet. And once I've clocked what time she's there, I make sure I'm out by that time so I don't have to bump into her again. I always leave a tip though, to show my thanks, of course.

When I open the patio door, I hear his voice. He appears from around the corner on the phone and puts it down.

'You made it down before your thirty minutes, and you look beautiful.'

'Why thank you. I'm going au naturel, being as though you told me to wear swimwear. Am I suitable?'

'Perfect,' he says as we sit at the table.

'You've been rumbled,' I say, taking a bite of my sandwich.

'What do you mean?' He has a look of panic in his face.

'Camila—' I point inside '—she's busy making the picnic, not you! Trying to take the credit for that poor woman's work. Tut, tut!' I say teasingly.

'Oh! Yes, sorry. I did start making it, honestly. My phone rang – work stuff, you know – and she ushered me out and took over. But the thought, that was all me!' he says with a dazzling smile.

'I'm only teasing! I don't care who makes it; it's very thought-ful. And I'm super excited to find out where we're going!'

We get out of the taxi in front of what looks like a marine park. 'Have you ever been swimming with dolphins?' he asks, taking me by the hand and leading me inside.

'No way!' I squeal, staring at him, eyes wide.

'Yes way!' he says, picking me up and spinning me around. 'I just love putting that big smile on your face.'

'You really don't need to pay for dolphins to get a smile on my face,' I say cheekily, 'but I'm so glad you did! I've always wanted to do this! Thank you!'

Once we're inside and checked in, we go to a changing room and strip down to our swimwear. Dumping all of our belongings in a locker, we make our way over to the poolside. I say pool –

it's the sea. It's as though they've sectioned off part of the sea for the dolphins.

Part of me feels a bit sad that this is the life they have. In captivity. Poor things. Then I spend some time convincing myself that they must be here because they couldn't survive in the wild for some reason, and that places like these are actually helping them.

I realise we're the only two people here. The dolphin trainer tells us her name is Sofia. We're issued with life jackets, and then we walk down the floating jetty and ease ourselves into the water.

First, she introduces a sea lion called Bob. He bounds over full of confidence swimming around us and giving us a wave before getting back on his pedestal to collect his reward of fish. He takes it gratefully and nods his head up and down in approval. He is such a character and so cute!

Next, she points her finger away from us and blows her whistle. He swims in the direction she has sent him, and then she hands us a ball. She says to throw it in his direction when she blows her whistle. As soon as she whistles, I chuck it, and he comes out of the water balancing the ball on his nose and parades around us in a circle showing off. Again, he's back to his pedestal for his fish while we applaud.

Alex has a turn, and again Bob balances the ball on his nose with ease. The next time she sends him over, he swims on his side with one flipper out of the water, and she tells us to give him a high five as he passes. Back on the pedestal, she tells him to take a bow and he does, then he claps and waves goodbye.

'That was so amazing!' I say to Alex, waving goodbye to Bob. 'How on earth do they get them to do these things?'

'A bucketload of fish, it seems!' he says, clapping and waving.

The trainer announces she's bringing out the dolphins, and she introduces them as Hannah and Hoya. She tells us about their anatomy and lets us stroke them as they swim past lying on their backs. They're so smooth. We are instructed to stroke the upper part of their undersides only, just as I'm approaching the lower part, otherwise we'll be touching the genital area. I quickly raise my hand.

After a few minutes of petting, and a lot of fish, she tells me to swim out to where a buoy is floating and to hold my arms out at my sides, and when the dolphins swim underneath my hands, to hold each of their dorsal fins and they'll pull me along in the water. I do as I'm told, although I'm wondering if this is going to work. What if I miss them? Once she blows the whistle, within seconds I can feel their fins beneath my hands! I hold on only gently, afraid of hurting these beautiful creatures. But they pull me along with such ease; they're so strong. I glide across the water with these magnificent creatures and I feel elated. As we reach where Alex and Sofia are waiting, they disappear under the water and leave me floating next to Alex with a massive grin on my face.

'Did you see that? How bloody awesome was that?' I say to Alex while watching the dolphins eat their fish.

'It was amazing! How did it feel?'

'Just like I was gliding along!'

Sofia tells Alex that it's his turn. Once he's in place, I watch waiting to see the reaction on his face the moment they appear beneath him. And there it is. He has massive boyish smile and he starts gliding towards us.

'That was bloody fantastic!' he roars as he comes to a stop next to me.

Sofia laughs. 'One more thing, guys, before we let these ladies get their rest. Would you like a kiss from one of them while we get your picture?'

'Absolutely!' I giggle and clap... I feel like I'm turning into Bob.

When we get outside, the taxi is waiting for us. Alex opens the car door. 'Ready for part two?'

'Ready!' I throw myself into the car and the welcoming air con. We are taken to a private beach. It's only tiny, but it's secluded; there is not another soul to be seen. We have our own little cove!

He puts down the picnic basket, throws out a blanket, removes his T-shirt and settles down on the cover. I remove my clothes and lie down next to him in my bikini, trying to subtly stretch it over my boobs to give maximum cleavage impact.

'How do you know about this little gem?' I ask him.

'It's lovely, isn't it? Beaches are always so much nicer when there's nobody else disturbing the view, don't you think?'

'Definitely. I think this is the first time I've experienced it, though!'

'Hungry?' he asks whilst pulling over the picnic basket.

'Famished!' I reply, excited to see what delights await us.

As he opens it up, he pulls out a bottle of champagne and two glasses. I realise now why we were in a taxi and not his car.

He pops the cork with a bang and pours us a glass each, then he hands me an ice-cold bottle of water. 'Keep hydrated, OK? It's hot today!' he orders.

'Yes, sir,' I say jokingly, saluting him. But I do take big gulp of water before sipping the champagne; I don't think I've ever had a champagne picnic before. Champagne seems to make everything feel so much more sophisticated.

He pulls out little food platters and removes the foil. There are mini baguettes, salad, roast chicken, different cheeses, watermelon and strawberries.

'Wow, that's quite a spread!' I say, shoving a cherry tomato in my mouth. Swimming always makes me feel starving. Not that I did much swimming myself, to be fair. I mean, the dolphins did all the hard work!

Alex pops a strawberry into each of our champagne glasses and makes us a chicken salad baguette each. We sit in comfortable silence for a while scoffing away looking out at the sea. It's so beautiful; we don't need to fill the space with words.

It doesn't matter how careful you are, whenever you eat on the beach, some sand manages to creep into your mouth. I can feel a bit of grit in my teeth. I swill with some water.

Afterwards, he handfeeds me watermelon. It's super juicy and perfect for washing down the sandwich, but the juice drips down my chin and I feel its stickiness. I dab it away with my arm hoping that Alex can't see it, and I return the favour by popping a strawberry into his mouth. He bites it so seductively. Unlike me – it was like trying to feed a toddler!

'That was such an amazing experience, Alex! Thank you so much! Dolphins are brilliant, aren't they? So intelligent!'

'Yes, it really was. I very much enjoyed seeing your face light up.' He pulls out the photos we had taken with the dolphins kissing our cheeks. 'This face, right here. Look at that smile. I'm going to make it my mission to keep that smile on your face every single day, Amy.'

'Well, I think you might be able to get a smile like that on my face without spending so much money!' I say cheekily. 'And this picnic, on this secluded beach, with champagne...it's all very romantic. It's just perfect, thank you.'

'Thank you, Amy, for staying out here with me. I know I'm asking a lot of you, taking you out of your comfort zone, but I'm really glad you stayed.'

'Me too.'

'Fancy a dip?'

'Yeah sure!' I start walking towards the sea and realise the sand is boiling and I have to hotfoot it to the sea whilst making noises akin to a chimpanzee. That was not the sultry walk I was trying to pull off, but then I notice he's doing the exact same goofy half-run behind me.

'Jesus that sand is hot!' he says as his feet splash into the sea.

'I know.' I giggle.

He hands me my drink and we sit on the seabed watching the sunlight dance over the water. He puts his arm around me, and I feel completely content.

We return to the villa in the early evening and decide to have another relaxing night in. I'm wiped out from all the day's activities. I settle down to finish the film from last night whilst he makes some calls. I plonk myself on the sofa with some of the leftover picnic and take a look at my phone. There are four texts.

First is from Mum: *Hi Amy, just checking you're ok? Hope you're still enjoying yourself without Steph? xx.*

Second is from Lauren: *Hi Amy. Missed you being back at work today! I don't want things to be weird just because you're with Alex. Keep in touch, let me know you're ok! xx.*

The third is Steph: *Hiya babe! It was SO gutting being back at work today! Text me and fill me in on all the details of your shagathon since I've been gone! Miss ya xxx.*

And the forth is Steph again: *And I miss the sun!! Bloody rain here, waaah! xx.*

I reply to everyone letting them know I'm fine and that I've had the best day ever and I will fill them in when I speak to them. Far too much has happened today to fit it all in a text message.

By the time Alex comes back in, the film's nearly over and I've demolished most of the food.

'Sorry about that,' he says, ruffling his hair and looking stressed.

'That's OK. You alright?'

'I'm fine. At least, I will be. What do you say to taking the rest of these strawberries and having a hot bath?'

'I say yes please!' I reply, jumping up from the sofa eagerly. I know we've been busy, but I feel a little hurt that we haven't had sex today. Which I know is ridiculous; he's planned the most romantic day I've ever had in my life! But for some reason I start getting worried that he doesn't want me, that maybe he's changed his mind, just because he doesn't want to rip my clothes off. Which would be deeply upsetting, because I've felt like I've wanted to rip his off all day! Now I know he still wants me, my day feels complete.

CHAPTER TWENTY-ONE

The next morning he's gone when I wake up. How does he do that? Sneak out all stealthlike without waking me up, like some sort of ninja. I think I've been in a deeper sleep since I've been here – maybe because I've been drunk half the time…but maybe because I'm happier now too! I look on the bedside cabinet for my cup and my note. Sure enough, they're both there. He's made me a latte, and it's still warm – bonus. The note reads:

Dearest Amy,

It pained me to leave your naked body lying in my bed this morning, but unfortunately work duty calls. I'll be back late afternoon.

Yours, Alex xx.

That is kind of perfect. As much as I'll miss him, I really could do with some me time. I need to shave, pluck my eyebrows and sort my toenails out. Things I can't do in front of a god of a man I've known less than a fortnight. Whilst I'm sitting in bed drinking my coffee, I decide to call Steph and fill her in now that he's not around to hear me gushing over him.

She answers after a couple of rings. 'Hi, beaut!'

'Hi, hon!'

'So, how are you coping without me?'

'Well, Alex has been extremely thoughtful in keeping me occupied, so I don't feel your absence too much!'

'I bet he has!'

I can't help but giggle. 'Not just in *that* way! OMG, Steph, yesterday I felt like someone out of a chick flick! First, he took me swimming with dolphins. Actual dolphins, can you believe it? Then we had a champagne picnic on a tiny little beach, and we were the only people there! The whole thing was so romantic!'

'Wow, it sounds it, babe! I can totally see why you're not missing me!'

'Oh, I am. Alex is out now, and I'm left here all alone, which feels weird. I think I might take a walk into the town, take a look at Prego, make some notes on my new project.'

'So, you done it in the pool yet?'

'Oh, sorry, am I boring you with work talk?' I tease.

'Yes! I'm at work. I need an escape. Tell me about rubbing oil into his chiselled abs or something, please!'

'Oh, Steph, sounds like you're one horny girl who needs to get some again!'

'Yes, I do. But I can't, so at least tell me all about yours! Oh, I have to go into a boring sales forecast meeting in five, babe.'

'No worries, you get off. I'll call again soon, OK.'

'OK, miss you, Ames!'

'Miss you too, Steph. Oh, and we already did it in the pool.'

I hear her laugh. 'You naughty, naughty girl! I hope it wasn't while I was still using it! Ew! Right, adios, speak soon!'

'Bye, honey!' I hang up the phone and smile to myself. Poor Steph is sat in a dull meeting room, and here I am in paradise. I am one lucky girl.

I stroll into the town checking my reflection in the windows as I pass. I think this new-found sex life is doing wonders for my figure. I'm wearing a wrap-around khaki dress and brown sandals, hair up in a top knot, with oversized shades and blinged up with a bit of jewellery. I'm not sure the restaurant actually knows what I'm going to be doing, but I want to look presentable just in case Alex has filled them in.

As I approach Prego, I pull out my lip gloss and swipe it over my lips. I sit at the same table as last time so I get a whole view of the restaurant and pull out a notepad I found in Alex's kitchen drawer. I order a Fanta Limón and start making notes, and little sketches. I wonder if we could get the sign replaced outside too. Its tacky neon sign screams cheap pizza joint, whereas I want it to say quaint, family-run bistro. I sketch out a few ideas. I wonder if I can find some inspiration by checking out the other restaurants and maybe some shops. The shops tend to just sell touristy tat or clothes, though. I decide to have wander.

After paying the bill, I start walking down the main strip. I feel so exhilarated. I'm in this beautiful country in the glorious sunshine, I have a drop-dead gorgeous boyfriend and now I have a new job that is something I actually enjoy! And I have a feeling I'm going to be quite good at it. I stop at the first restaurant I find with clean, crisp white tablecloths and pretend to read the menu board, when I'm actually checking out their signage, plants, ornaments and tableware. But then I look up and notice Mia sat at one of the tables facing me. Shit. She hasn't seen me yet. I can't help but stare at her, checking out the ex-competition.

Suddenly, I see Alex approach the table. He sits opposite her. I duck behind the board; I can feel my heart thumping in my chest. What. The. Fuck. I sneak a peek and he's sat with his back to me, so I brave standing up to get a better view. Mia's eyes flick to mine and hold my gaze for a couple of seconds before she pulls Alex towards her and kisses him intently.

I feel the tears sting my eyes and my whole world comes crashing down. I run down the street, and as soon as I see a taxi, I jump in and ask him to take me back to the villa. My tears are streaming down my face; I feel like I can hardly breathe. The taxi driver keeps looking at me concerned, but I bury my face in my hands.

When I'm safely back in the villa, I sob and scream until there's nothing left. I'm so confused. He seemed so genuine. Why all the romance if I was just a fling? Why convince me to stay, give me a job, when he could have just had what he wanted and sent me back home?

Maybe I was just a rebound. Maybe she's only just called him, and he's agreed to get back together. And maybe he's coming home to tell me that he doesn't want me any more. Hang on – the signs have been there. The disappearing when talking on the phone. I knew it was too good to be true! It was all too bloody perfect!

I look in the mirror at my red puffy eyes and tell myself to pull it together. Oh Amy, you've been such a fool. I go to the sink and splash my face with cold water, which feels soothing on my burning eyes. I take some paracetamol for the pounding head-ache that's appeared from all the crying. I then run upstairs and pack my things. I can't face him. I can't stand to look at him. I'll just go home and forget this holiday ever happened; he can go back to Moody Mia. Good luck to him.

I'm channelling my sadness into anger now, and everything is being thrown into my case with grunts and screams. I call a taxi to take me to the airport and finish packing my things. I try calling Steph a few times, but it goes straight to voicemail. She's probably still in her meeting. I leave his notepad on the side and consider writing him a note. I try to talk myself out of it – but the longer I wait for the taxi, the more things I find I have to say to him. As I flip past all my sketches, I'm upset that I won't be able to make them a reality any more. I decide to keep the note brief, but to let him know how hurt I am. He has to know. He can't just do this to people. Mess with their minds. Get their hopes up. For nothing.

Alex

I was stupid and naïve to think this was actually going some-where. I was actually falling for you. How could you? I hope you and Mia are very happy together!

Amy

Writing this makes me remember his notes. I run back up-stairs and grab them. I can't bring myself to part with them. Although right now I feel like he's a complete bastard, I need to hang on to the memory. The taxi pulls up and I take one last glance around the villa, sadness tugging at my chest.

When I get to the airport, I start questioning if I'm doing the right thing. I don't even know when the next flight is. I could be here for bloody hours. I drag my case around not even sure where I need to go. Do I go to a check-in desk? Do I need to go somewhere else to book?

As I'm wandering aimlessly, I notice a flight on the Ryanair check-in screen that's going home in forty-five minutes. I scramble over all flustered and ask the check-in lady if I can book a seat. She tells me there are a few spaces left, and that I need to book online and come back with a boarding pass. I fumble around on my phone checking it's the right flight and time. Bloody expensive. Last-minute travel used to be cheaper than if you booked ahead, didn't it? It seems to have taken me ages to get this far, and now I'm panicking that I'll miss the flight if I deliberate any longer. I just need to get home. I pay and quickly navigate to download my boarding pass.

Back at the desk, I show the lady my screen. She takes the phone from me and scans it before checking my passport and weighing my bag. 'All done,' she announces.

'Thank you!' I run over to the security queue frantically checking my watch. Why are the queues for security always so long when you're abroad? My mind is reeling. Maybe I should have heard him out before I ran off. There's nothing to explain really, is there? You witnessed the kiss. He lied and said he had work to do. He ditched your naked body in bed to go and smooch Mia and patch things up. It's over. Get over it. Shit.

In my daydream, I didn't realise that I was next and I'm now holding up the queue. I can hear people tutting and grumbling behind me. Usually, I'd be politely apologising – I usually say sorry when something isn't even my fault, like someone else walking into me – but right now, I'm not in the mood. I throw them dirty looks and, to my surprise, they quickly look down at the ground.

I toss my bag onto the X-ray machine and walk through the scanner. The security guy pulls me over and eyes me suspiciously whilst waving the wand over my arms and legs. I realise this is not the place to be moody. These guys can put latex-covered fingers where you really don't want them. I offer a weak, feeble smile; his frown eases as he nods that I can go. Phew!

Grabbing my bag, I scan the screen for the boarding details

and make a run for the gate. There are a couple of people left to get on, so I stand behind them trying to get my breath back. I'm still questioning myself if I'm doing the right thing. What else could I do?

Once safely seated on the plane, I notice a few people looking over at me. I pull out my mirror and soon realise exactly what they're looking at. I look terrible. But who can blame me? Sod what they think. I don't care what they think. They can all just leave me the hell alone. I type a quick text to Steph: *Coming home! Meet me at the airport please? Taking off shortly xxx.* I then turn off my phone and shove my bag back under the seat. As soon as we're in the air, I order four gin and tonics. They will get me through the flight.

CHAPTER TWENTY-TWO

We come into land, and the man sitting next to me looks relieved. Poor guy. I've been boring him with my tales of woe for the last four hours. He really has tried his best to ignore me and read his book. I start crying again as soon as the wheels hit the tarmac. I don't want to be home! Everyone is going to think I was so stupid. Thinking I could stay there with some dream guy and ditch everything.

As soon as I turn on my phone, it starts pinging like mad. I squint to see the screen. Six missed calls from Steph. Eighteen missed calls from Alex. Texts notifications start bleeping.

Steph: *OMG babe what's happened? xx.*

Steph: *Fuck, you're in flight already aren't you! Can't get through! X.*

Alex: *Amy, it's not what you think. Where have you gone? Please come back, let's talk about this xx.*

Alex: *Amy please, don't do this! xxx.*

I put the phone in my lap and stare out of the window. Grey skies. Rain spitting. Sums up my mood.

'So, have you heard from him?' asks random guy next to me. Ah, I must have piqued his interest after all. I show him the messages. 'That doesn't sound like a guy that wants to end it, to me.'

'It's a bit late now though, isn't it!' I scoff.

'Well, from what you've told me, you didn't really give him a chance to explain anything. Do you run from a relationship as soon as things get tough?'

'There really is no explanation for cheating scumbag though, is there?'

'I just think maybe you should have heard what he had to say before you hopped on a plane home. Innocent until proven guilty, and all that.'

'Thanks, but…I saw it with my own eyes! Guilty was written

159

all over their pretty, cheating little faces!' He hands me a second packet of tissues, as I had used up the pack he gave to me earlier. 'Thanks,' I say, taking them, wondering what kind of man carries tissues around. I'm grateful, though. I really hope Steph is meeting me here. I need to vent to someone who knows the situation – to someone who will be on my side.

After finally coming through baggage and passport control, I amble through the Nothing to Declare tunnel. I search for Steph's familiar face amongst the other people gathered to greet expected arrivals. There she is! I've spotted her. I wave and stumble over my ankle. I quickly pick myself up again, limping a little and hoping nobody else noticed.

'Jesus, you OK?' she asks, taking my arm in hers. 'You look a little...dishevelled?'

'Dishevelled?'

'That's the polite word for you look like crap.'

'Thanks!'

'Is your ankle OK?'

'Just a little sore. Could we maybe go to a bar and just sit for a little bit?'

'I have to drive, and you look like you've had a few already. Let's get us a nice Costa for now, eh? I can totally get drunk with you later, I know you're going to be in full-on destruction mode given the circumstances, but I need you sober first so you can tell me all about it accurately.'

'OK,' I grumble.

Once she's ordered our drinks in the café, she comes over to our table and places a large latte in front of me, along with a chocolate doughnut.

I instantly burst out crying, and she tries to shush me whilst stroking my hair and handing me napkins. 'Take the doughnut away please – it reminds me of Alex. The floating doughnut, in the pool!'

'Oh crap,' she says, turning away and shoving it into her mouth. She turns back around with big hamster-like cheeks and chocolate all over her lips. 'Done!' she announces, showing me her empty hands as proof, as if I couldn't see that it was all stuffed in her mouth.

I laugh. 'I'm sorry. I know that is very pathetic of me.'

'Honey, you're allowed to be! Just tell me exactly what happened.'

I relay the whole story to Steph whilst choking back the sobs.

'Well, babe, I can certainly see why you're upset. But do you not think you should've given him a chance to explain before getting the first flight home?'

'You sound like the random on the plane! I thought you'd have my back!'

'Course I have your back. One hundred per cent! But Alex seemed so perfect. I just couldn't picture him doing this to you. I saw what he was like with you, what the pair of you were like! My little smitten kittens! Remember? It just doesn't make sense.'

'I didn't think so either, Steph, but I saw it with my own bloody eyes!'

'OK, keep calm. Deep breath. Now, don't freak out, OK?'

'What do you mean, don't freak out?'

'There's a lady walking this way and waving, and I think it might be Lauren.'

'What? Why would it be Lauren?'

'Because I called her on the way.'

'What?!'

'Come on, I'm sorry, I had to speak to someone. I don't have Alex's number. I was trying to figure out what was going on!'

Lauren walks straight over and hugs me. Her hair smells so nice and clean. I realise I don't smell very nice at all. I probably smell as good as I look.

'Amy, I'm so sorry. What's happened? You must be Steph?' She turns to Steph, and they both exchange a hug.

'I'll get you a coffee and you can hear her story,' says Steph whilst standing up.

'Sure, Americano, please. Thanks.' Lauren sits in Steph's seat and takes my hand. 'Tell me everything, Amy.'

I feel emotionally drained retelling the story for the third time. Lauren just listened intently and didn't say anything apart from the occasional 'uh-huh' to encourage me to continue. I had to dial back the hatred a bit, it being her brother and all.

'OK, firstly, we're going to get you cleaned up, because it's obvious you've shed a lot of tears over my idiot brother, and I think you could use a nice long hot bath. OK, hon?'

'OK.' I nod. I know I look a state.

'I'm also not going to make excuses for my idiot brother. However, I know Mia – and I know she's a manipulative bitch. So, would you at least hear Alex out? For me?'

'Sure.' How can I deny my boss? I'm going to need her rubbish job now, aren't I?

'Steph, are you OK to join us?' asks Lauren when she returns with her coffee.

'Yeah, the only thing I had planned this evening was getting drunk with this one,' she says, pulling me up into a hug.

'Well, that is definitely part of the plan, Steph!' Lauren replies with a wink.

Lauren pulls into a large tree-lined driveway off a country lane. I should have known her house would be massive as well.

Steph's following in her car and parks up next to us. 'Nice digs!' she shouts whilst getting out.

'Thanks,' says Lauren. 'Come on in.'

We enter the huge hallway, which has wooden floors and white walls, other than one wall which is a bold blue colour. Large pieces of artwork line the walls along with a huge ornate mirror. I catch a glimpse of my reflection; I see what everyone's been complaining about.

'Come on, honey.' Lauren takes my hand and starts up the stairs. 'Follow me. Bring your case up so you can get changed after. Steph, go through to the lounge and make yourself at home.'

I pick my case up, trying not to bash it against the wooden stairs. I follow her across the landing and into a bedroom.

'You can stay here tonight, unless you wanted to go home?' says Lauren.

'Here's good, thanks, if you don't mind,' I say, placing my case on the bed. I open it and everything inside is screwed up.

Lauren gasps. 'My God, you're a messy packer!'

'No, I was just packing in haste, remember!'

'Pick something out. I'll iron it for you while you get washed up.'

'There's no need – it's fine.'

'There's every need, trust me. Pick something.' I pass her a plain yellow maxi dress, but she hands it back. 'Pick something nicer?'

'Are we going somewhere?'

'Maybe.'

I pick up a short black dress and raise my eyebrows awaiting approval.

'Can't go wrong with an LBD! Follow me, I'll show you the bathroom.' I follow her to the end of the landing. There's a large stand-alone bath on a raised platform and she turns on the waterfall tap. She opens a cupboard and pulls out various bottles. She picks one up and tips it in. 'Essential oil – it'll make your skin feel super soft,' she explains. 'The others are for you to use when you're in there. This one, though, is moisturiser for after. You have a great tan; keep it moisturised to make it last longer. When was the last time you ate?'

'Er...this morning.'

'Right, I'll fix us a quick snack and get your dress ironed. You, relax. And help yourself to a towel when you're done, OK? And don't worry. I'm sure we can fix whatever this misunderstanding is.'

'OK.' When she leaves the room, I feel all alone, and full of heartache again. The anger has gone; I'm just miserable again. The bath fills quickly, and I climb in and submerge my head under the water. The last time I was like this, Alex walked in and saw me naked. I pull myself up out of the water and scrape the bubbles off my face and out of my hair. I hug my knees and cry.

When I get back into the room, Steph's waiting for me. 'Feeling better, babe?'

'Not really. I'm still upset, and now I'm sober.'

'Right, you get yourself dry and in that sexy little number hanging up there. I'll go and get you a drinkypoo, OK?'

'OK.' She totters off downstairs. Why are they making me get ready to go out? It's the last thing I want to do. They should know that. Steph should know that. I just want to sit around in joggers eating my bodyweight in chocolate and wallowing in my own self-pity. Preferably whilst getting smashed.

I sit on the bed and start moisturising my legs. This must be expensive; it feels gorgeous. I rub it in all over and wrap the towel back around me just in time for Steph to come in wielding cocktails. Now that looks like something I want to take part in. I rub the excess lotion off my hands onto the towel before taking the glass off her. I do not want to be spilling this orange-coloured drink on her plush cream carpet.

'Pornstar Martini,' says Steph, taking a sip. 'Bloody delicious.'

I take a sip. 'Mmm...that is really yummy,' I agree. I shuffle up the bed and rest my back against the headboard enjoying my drink.

Steph climbs on the bed and sits next to me. 'We can sit and enjoy these for five, but then we need to get you ready.'

'What for?'

'You'll see.'

'I really can't be arsed to go out, Steph.'

'You will love it, trust me. And stop feeling like it's the end of the world, because whatever it is, I'm sure there's a reasonable explanation, and you guys will be back together before you know it.'

I roll my eyes and get back to drinking my delightful cocktail. For five minutes I can just indulge in this and forget everything else.

Drinks down, Steph is now drying my hair and applying my make-up. She plugs in the straighteners and orders me to get dressed. I step into the dress, and she pulls up the zip before sitting me back on the stool.

'No peeking until my masterpiece is complete.' She sprays each strand of my hair with something before running the straighteners over it, and my hair glistens with shine. Whatever that stuff is, I need to buy some. It's helping my hair not having the humidity, I guess. Although, I'd prefer to be in the heat with my frizzy hair. Try not to think about it. Eye make-up will smudge, and Steph won't be amused. The last time Steph did my hair and make-up was for my big date with Alex. Don't think about it. Don't think about it. Don't think about it.

'Are you crying again?' she asks. Damn.

'Sorry, Steph.'

'Don't be sorry. Just try to stop crying for a little bit, OK. I'm surprised you have any water left inside you.' She dabs my cheek with a tissue, reapplies some make-up and gets back to my hair. 'You're going to speak to Alex soon and get to hear his side of the story, OK. So just try not to fret until you've spoken to him and you know what the craic is, alright?'

'Are we having a Skype call? Is that what this is all in aid of?'

'Close your eyes and mouth now – hairspray time.'

I do as I'm told. When the spraying stops, I open my eyes. She shows me my reflection, and I'm amazed. 'Aw, you can't even see my puffy eyes.'

'Yes, I worked very hard to cover all that up, so please don't cry again! Now, get your shoes on and come downstairs.'

'I'm still not sure.'

'You don't want another Pornstar Martini, then?'

'OK, I'm coming!' The shoes she has put out for me are the

shoes she gave me. *The* shoes. I try to put it to the back of my mind and put them on. Then she spritzes me with my perfume. The one that drives him wild. And I have to hold back another sob.

When we enter the kitchen, there are three Pornstar Martinis on the side along with some snacks. Lauren skips over. 'Oh, wow, you look absolutely killer!'

'Thanks, Steph's handiwork.' I shrug. We all pick up our drinks and stand sipping in silent appreciation.

'Right, I'm going to quickly tart myself up. Be back down in ten minutes, ladies. Make sure you eat some of those snacks to keep you going, Amy – you smell absolutely gorge, by the way!' says Lauren, placing her empty glass on the counter.

'Oh shit, I need to get myself ready,' says Steph as she pulls her hair out of her ponytail and ruffles her hair. She opens her handbag and blasts her hair with hairspray. Then she pulls out some eyeshadow, which she dabs on with her fingers before rinsing them under the tap, and then she slaps on some lipstick. How can someone go from office chic to out on the town in five minutes? Only Steph could pull that off.

Five minutes later, Lauren walks down the stairs looking completely glamorous. OK, maybe only Steph and Lauren can pull that off. She's wearing a floor-length gown, plain but elegant.

'Let's go, girls!' calls Lauren, heading straight to the front door.

There's a taxi waiting outside. Where the hell are they taking me?

CHAPTER TWENTY-THREE

'Where the hell are we?' I ask when the taxi pulls up. It's a hotel. Why are they bringing me to a hotel?

'We're at a work shindig,' says Lauren.

'Work?' I ask, confused.

'Well, it's an award ceremony. It'll be a bit boring, but they always make it more exciting by getting a comedian to host it, so it'll be a good laugh. And, it's a free bar. Happy now?'

'It's sounding more appealing,' I admit, 'but I'd still rather just be lounging at home, if I'm honest.'

'Trust me, babe, Lauren's dragging you out for good reason,' says Steph.

After walking into the hotel, we are shown into a function room. It's actually looks very nice. You wouldn't know we were sat in a hotel. There are white silky drapes lining every wall with fairy lights hanging over them. There are large round tables with white tablecloths and big silver candelabras with a sprinkling of diamantés. Normally, I'd think candelabras look dated, but the way the rest of the room is decorated, it just looks classy.

'I feel like we're at a wedding reception,' whispers Steph.

'Girls, I have some mingling to do,' says Lauren. 'Here are your wristbands. Pop them on and get yourself to the bar. Oh, and get me one, would you?'

'Course!' says Steph, taking the wristbands and marching me up to the bar.

'Any idea who the comedian is?' I ask.

'Oh yeah, it's David Manton! He is hilarious! We might even be able to get a selfie later!' I nod my head and focus back on the bar. 'Sorry, I forgot you're feeling shitty and not excited about this in the slightest, but you don't have long to wait now.'

'Why do I have to wait so long to speak to him? Can't we just ring him and get it over with?'

'Three glasses of Prosecco, please,' she says to the barman. 'Prosecco OK, babe?'

'Yeah sure.' I turn around and see that people are starting to take their seats. My tummy is rumbling although I have no appetite. I wonder if I should've forced down some of Lauren's snacks earlier. 'I think we need to be sitting down,' I say, taking my drink.

'Oh yeah, Lauren's over there. Let's go see.'

Lauren spots us across the room, waves and then points to some seats at the table in front of her.

As we sit down, people are being served soup and bread rolls. Thank God for that. Something to soak up this alcohol.

The soup was enough for me to be honest. I have been pushing the stuffed chicken and potatoes around my plate for the last twenty minutes pretending to be eating. I'm sat in the middle of Lauren and Steph, protected from having to talk to randoms I can't be bothered with. I just look up every now and then and smile, as if I'm listening to their conversation. Finally, my plate is taken away, but no sooner are they back with dessert.

'Bar?' I say to Steph.

She nods and excuses herself. 'Are you OK, you hardly ate a thing, Ames?'

'What do you expect, Steph? This time yesterday, I was in paradise having the best day of my life with a gorgeous, thoughtful, romantic man. Today I'm back home, and it's all over!'

'Don't say it's over yet, not before you've heard him out.'

'Three?' asks the barman, holding the Prosecco bottle.

Steph nods to him and tucks my hair behind my ear. 'OK, hon, nothing is over yet, so don't go thinking like that.'

Although I'm pretty sure it's over – I've fled the country, after all, and left without hearing him out – her words are still soothing and help me to hold back the tears.

'Actually, make that six?' Steph asks the barman.

He sighs, puts the three glasses he's already poured onto a

tray, which he hands to Steph, and then hands me the rest of the bottle.

'Thanks! You're a star!' Steph says, air-kissing in his direction. That puts an instant shy smile on his face. I have a feeling she'll just be given the bottle next time!

We get back to the table with the drinks and Lauren greets us with a smile.

'David Manton is coming on in five minutes, girls, so it's toilet break time, you coming?'

'Yeah sure.' We place down our drinks, pick up our bags and follow Lauren to the toilet.

After a quick wee, we're all standing in front of the mirror washing our hands, topping up make-up and smoothing hair.

'Lauren, darling,' comes a voice from behind, 'don't you three all look absolutely stunning! Who are your friends?'

'Mum!' says Lauren, and I suddenly feel awkward.

She doesn't even know who I am, I think to myself. She's as elegant as her daughter, wearing a long gown with long lace sleeves. Her grey bob doesn't have a hair out of place, and her make-up is flawless and subtle.

'This is Amy, she works with us, and this is her friend Stephanie.'

'Amy, a pleasure to meet you,' she says, shaking my hand.

'Nice to meet you, Mrs Stevenson,' I say timidly. Mums of boyfriends always intimidate me. Management people intimidate me. This is a double whammy! She holds my gaze for a while, and I wonder if she knows.

Then she moves on to shake Steph's hand. 'Stephanie, pleasure.'

'Hi, Mrs Stevenson.'

'Girls, my name is Edith. You'd better hurry along, the comedian is about to come on, so I'm told.'

'See you later, Mum,' says Lauren, kissing her on the cheek as we all file out of the ladies.

As we get back to the table, I take my seat and down my Prosecco. Steph doesn't say a word; she just tops me back up again.

No judgement. I love that girl. The lights dim and we swivel our seats around to face the stage.

The comedian has been quite entertaining; it would have been terribly dull otherwise. I wondered why we weren't on the same table as Lauren's parents, but Lauren explained that they mix the companies so everyone gets a chance to mingle and network.

I'm laughing at something the comedian says when I scan the room looking for Edith and checking out what Lauren's dad looks like. Not to check out in *that* way. But if I know what he looks like, I can try to avoid making a fool of myself in front of him later.

Then I catch him staring at me from the back of the room. Alex. It's bloody Alex.

He's leaning against the wall, hands in his pockets, with a pained look on his face. I can't look away. I'm just stunned, pinned to the spot. Everyone's laughing and Steph nudges me. I look up and realise that everyone's staring.

'Alright, love?' asks the comedian. 'Something more interesting over there, is there, than watching my act? Well, it wouldn't take much, I suppose!'

The audience laugh, but I'm mortified. I hate being the centre of attention.

He steps down and looks over in the same direction I was looking. 'Can't say I blame you, darlin'! He's a bit of alright, isn't he?'

I keep looking at the floor, refusing to make eye contact with this guy so he can ridicule me some more. When I dare to glance up at Alex, he looks equally as embarrassed. He holds my gaze again immediately.

'Woah, I think you pair need to get a room! Luckily for you, you're in just the place! Can someone get these pair a room, please?' says the comedian, chuckling to himself as he clambers back onto the stage.

Perfect. His parents and his sister are in the room. Ground, swallow me up, please. Steph passes me a full glass of Prosecco with a rub of the shoulder. That'll do.

I don't even listen to what the comedian says for the next twenty minutes. Every now and then, I steal another glance; and as far as I can tell, he hasn't looked away from me once. At least now I know why they dragged me out and made sure I was looking fantastic.

As soon as the comedian has left the stage, I look at Alex and he tilts his head to say 'this way'. When he sees me stand up and walk towards him, he turns and walks through the door.

As I enter the hotel reception, I see that he's holding the main door open, waiting for me to go outside with him. He turns around to look at me, a pleading puppy dog look in his eyes, in his gorgeous (no doubt designer) grey suit, and the butterflies in my tummy are flapping around like crazy.

I walk over and through the door into the cool night air. Straight away, his jacket is off and around my shoulders. I get a waft of his aftershave and inhale it with my eyes closed. That smell is divine, the smell of Alex. When I open my eyes, he's stood in front of me. Crisp white shirt, nipples slightly showing through in the cold, and looking so damn sexy.

'Amy, you look...' He shakes his head slowly. 'Stunning, incredible...just, ah.' He bites his knuckle, and I can't help but feel satisfied that I do that to him. 'And those shoes, you know what those shoes do to me.'

I could tell him he's doing the exact same thing to me right now, that my body is aching for him, but I don't. I stand my ground, with a pissed off look on my face, defiant. 'You can't pretend like nothing happened, Alex.'

His face falls and goes back to serious mode. 'I know, Amy, but please listen. She kissed *me*. I didn't kiss her. After she kissed me, I pushed her off me, and then she started laughing hysterically. I didn't understand what she was laughing at until I got back and found your note. I was devastated. Honestly, I never did anything to hurt you. It was all Mia!'

'Why were you meeting your *ex* in the first place?' I demanded. I hated to sound like the jealous type, but I had to know.

'I said before, things with Mia, they're complicated. *We're* complicated. I told her, after that little stunt she pulled, she's on her own. Me and Mia have been on and off for years. But I was with her out of pity lately, not love. Lauren caught her stealing from the business. A few grand. It was taken out gradually over the years. I guess she thought she wouldn't get caught that way. But Lauren caught her, and I was ready to finish things then, but soon after, she rings me up in tears. She'd been raped, by some drunken thug, so I had to let the theft slide. I had to be there for her. Lauren didn't understand. She fell out with both of us. Mia's never been mentally stable anyway. She's had it tough, and the rape really affected her mental state. Whenever I tried to break it off with her, she threatened to harm herself. It's been very stressful, but I've tried my best to be there for her. And that situation I had to deal with, she was in the hospital. Overdose. I don't want to be with Mia, I promise you. I have been in this Mia world of torment for so long, trying to do the right thing by her, but she's never been appreciative of it. She just expects it. And then you came along. And I knew I had to be with you. It was time for Mia to learn to stand on her own two feet. I've just been trying to ease her into the transition, making sure she was OK mentally, trying to be supportive. There's nothing between us. You...you are everything. I see you and I feel things I didn't know I could feel. I...I know it's early days, but it's been so intense. I feel like I'm falling for you. I don't want to lose you, Amy.'

'And all the phone calls, were they Mia?'

'Yes, I was trying to tell her it was over; I told her about you. That's why I went to meet her, to try and sort it out once and for all, because she kept calling. She wouldn't take it.'

I walk over, pull his face down to mine and kiss him deeply.

After a couple of minutes, he pulls back and studies my face.

'You forgive me?'

'The way I see it, there's nothing to forgive. You've just proven once again what a wonderful person you are. Selfless. Strong. Supportive. And I think I'm falling for you too.'

He half laughs, half smiles and his eyes dance. 'Really?'

'Really,' I reply.

He kisses me now.

As soon as I can bring myself to, I pull back and look him in the eyes. 'Do you forgive me, Alex? For jumping on a plane and coming home the second things got tough?'

'I completely understand why you did it. As long as it's not a regular occurrence...'

'Absolutely not! I'm so sorry, sorry I dragged you back to England. I should've stayed and listened to what you had to say. I just panicked!'

'That's OK. My parents wanted me to come back for this thing anyway. They'll be pleased.'

'Oh, I met your mum.'

'Did you now? And how did that go?'

'It was just a quick hello.'

'I'm sure she'll get more out of you than a quick hello before the evening's out.'

'Oh dear, I've probably had far too much Prosecco for meeting the parents.' I giggle.

'It's an open bar, Amy. I bet my parents are wasted by now too!'

We kiss again, and everything feels right with the world again.

'Oh, found each other, did you? I could see you were dying to do that to each other all night!' It's the comedian walking to his car. We both laugh, and I bury my head in Alex's jacket. 'Young love, eh! Night, you two!'

'Night!' we call back, laughing.

'Shall we go back in?' asks Alex.

'Sure,' I say, handing back his jacket.

After the boring awards were over, the party was in full swing. Me, Alex, Steph and Lauren were up and down on the dance floor like yo-yos, only dancing to the music we knew and sitting out whenever something older came on, like Abba. It was a request DJ, so everyone was putting in their requests, and there was about a fifty-fifty split of the older generation and our generation in the room.

When Cher's 'If I Could Turn Back Time' comes on, we all meander back to the table. I'm quite glad of the breaks, it gives me a chance to cool off, so I don't turn into a big sweaty mess.

Edith Stevenson, and I assume her husband, come over to our table. Alex stands up and hugs them both before introducing me. If they didn't know who I was before, they must surely know who I am now they've seen me grinding up to their son on the dance floor. Shit. I forgot they were witnessing that. Hopefully they weren't looking.

'Mum, Dad, this is Amy. Amy, my mum you already met, Edith. And my dad, Graham.'

I stand up and shake their hands, but Graham pulls me in for a hug, much to my surprise!

'Welcome to the family, Amy! I've not seen my son this happy in years. Whatever it is you're doing, keep doing it!'

'Dad!' grumbles Alex, and I giggle.

'He has a point, Alex. Mia made you miserable. I've been watching this one. I think she'll fit in nicely. And with Mia out of the picture, my family can reunite as one again, can't they, Lauren!' says Edith.

'Yes, Mum, absolutely. I only hated that bitch face Mia. Amy is lovely. Amy can be my sister-in-law any day!'

'Lauren!' mutters Alex. 'I apologise, Amy, she's wrecked!'

'That's OK.' I laugh. I was nervous to meet these people. Well-off, management types. I expected them to be stuck up, and hostile. How wrong was I?

They join us at our table and Steph pours them a glass of Prosecco. The barman brings her a new bottle every time she waves in his direction.

'Richard!' Lauren shouts, waving her arms. A tall blond-haired man with a pleasant smile comes over and kisses her on the head.

'Oh dear, who got my wife drunk?' he asks, eyeing the suspects at the table.

Steph raises her hand. 'Me, your honour! I'm so sorry!'

He laughs. 'Well, it seems you're all rather on the same level? I had better play catch up!'

'Richard, this is Amyyyy! My new sister!' slurs Lauren.

'Hi!' I wave across to him.

He waves back. 'The famous Amy. Pleasure to meet you.' *Famous?* 'Alex, long time!' he says, saluting him. Alex salutes back.

'I'm Steph!' shouts Steph. 'Being as though no one wants to introduce me, I'll just introduce myself!'

'Shit, sorry, Steph!' says Lauren, hugging her head.

Rhianna comes on, and we all jump up and run to the dance floor, leaving Edith and Graham laughing at the table. They watch us all dancing around like fools and applaud us.

CHAPTER TWENTY-FOUR

I open my eyes and look around the room trying to figure out where I am. My head hurts so much that I daren't lift it off the pillow. Pale grey walls. Chandelier. Luxurious cream carpet. Mirrored bedside cabinet. Ooh…water. I decide the need for water outweighs the pain in my head, and I push myself up to a sitting position. I grab the water and gulp it down. I hope this is real and not another dream. I've dreamt about waking up and getting a glass of water four times.

Realising it's Lauren's house, I turn to see if Alex is next to me, but he's not there. Stealth ninja strikes again. I hate it when he leaves me in bed. Shit. He did come back here, didn't he? It's all a bit hazy. We made up; I remember that much.

It was all Moody Mia's fault. I feel bad calling her that now I know she's had mental health problems. Malicious Mia. There. I can call her that. Or bitch. I really shouldn't have got on a plane. Overreaction, or what. I'm kind of glad I did, though. It was such a laugh last night. Alex's mum and dad are so much fun, so laid back.

Alex walks in disturbing my thoughts with tray of food and orange juice, and a flower stem in between his teeth. He kicks the door shut with his foot and walks over to the bed.

I clap happily. 'You are my bloody hero, Alex Stevenson! Is that bacon I can smell?'

'Yes, bacon baps for milady,' he says after throwing the flower in my direction. I laugh. 'Paracetamol, milady?' he asks, handing me two capsules and kissing me gently on the lips.

'Ah yes, thank you. You know me so well already!' I neck the tablets followed by water and move straight on to the bap. It's massive, and just what I need this morning. The bacon is so thick and tasty. Proper bacon from the butchers, I can tell, not the thin crappy stuff from the supermarket.

'I love the appreciative sounds you make while you eat your food.' Alex laughs whilst also stuffing his face with a bacon bap.

'Sorry, I didn't realise I was oohing and aahing!' I say through a mouthful of bacon.

'It's fine. It's making me think of the noises you'll be making the moment you've finished your breakfast,' he says with a glint in his eye.

'Oh! Are those noises similar? I suppose I do love my food. So, that's the reason for breakfast in bed, is it? To keep me here for longer?'

'It certainly is.'

I eat the rest as quickly but as ladylike as I can manage before licking my fingers clean.

'What are you doing to me, Amy?' he says as I lick my finger.

'Sorry, I didn't realise I was doing anything erotic.' I laugh. 'You *are* a feeder, aren't you? I knew it!'

'A what-er?'

I neck my juice, and he takes the tray and places it on the floor. 'A feeder! Do you get turned on watching me eat and get fat?' I tease.

'No, I get turned on by you making groaning noises and licking things with that tantalising tongue!' he says as he throws his clothes on the floor and climbs back into bed.

About an hour and three triumphant moments later, we lie in a sweaty entangled embrace. 'Make-up sex is bloody marvellous,' I say with ragged breath.

'Yes, that felt as magical as the first time I explored your body. But don't go thinking that's a reason to fall out!' he warns, wagging a finger at me. 'Because that was the most horrendous time of my life. I thought I'd lost you.'

I pick up his hand and press my lips to it. 'Same. I was a right state. I don't wanna feel like that again.'

There's a knock on the door. Alex quickly pulls the quilt over us and says, 'Come in.'

Steph pokes her head around the door. 'You two lovebirds finished now?' she asks brazenly.

'Oh no, did you hear us? How embarrassing!' I pull the quilt over my head.

'Yeah, I heard. Quite the stallion, Alex. Everything Amy says is true, then!' She laughs, and I hide further down the quilt. 'I'm only teasing, Ames! Well, I did hear a little, but I've been next door getting ready. I'm sure no one else heard!'

Phew. I remove the cover from my head. 'Should you have been at work today?' I ask Steph.

'Yeah. *Bleurgh*. Had to bin it off. Told them I was hanging and that I'd book it as leave. They were fine. This is why I don't drink in the week!'

'It was a good night though, wasn't it?'

'Ah, it was awesome, babe! The night is always better when it's a free bar, don't you think?'

'Ahem.' Alex clears his throat.

'Sorry, is my presence making you feel uncomfortable while you're lying there in the buff, Alex?'

'Slightly,' he says. 'Maybe we can get ready and finish the conversation downstairs like normal people?' We laugh.

'This is totally normal! But fine, see you in a bit. I need coffee anyway,' she says, sticking her tongue out and closing the door behind her.

All showered and dressed, with the minimal amount of make-up applied so I look human, I go downstairs. Lauren's sprawled out on the sofa with a can of coke. Steph and Alex are on the opposite sofa.

'Here she is! Morning, Amy. How do you look so good?' asks Lauren, sitting up to make room.

'Shower and make-up!' I declare whilst sitting next to her.

'And some world-rocking make-up sex!' says Steph.

I hide my face with my hand.

'Ew! Stephanie! That's my *brother*, remember!'

'Oh crap. Soz, Lauren!' Steph clasps her hand to her mouth.

'I'm so glad you guys made up though, honestly. It was a surprise at first finding out about you two, but the more I thought about it, the more I thought how perfect you are for each other. I'm so happy you're together!' says Lauren.

'Yes, I gathered that last night, when you introduced her to everyone as your *sister-in-law*!' Alex reminds her.

'Oh God. I'm so sorry about that, Amy! I blame Steph for plying us with all that Prosecco!'

'It's fine!' I laugh. 'Yes, I think we all blame Steph for supplying us with all that Prosecco! I feel like death today.'

'Well, none of ya were complaining last night while I was keeping your glasses topped up, were ya?' We all laugh.

'Where's Richard?' I ask Lauren.

'He had to go to work. He didn't drink anywhere near what we drank – so don't worry, he was fine to drive! The downside to that is, he'll remind me of every stupid little thing I did last night and make me cringe! He said you were nice, though; I think the whole family approve!' she says, grinning at Alex.

'Oh well, I'm glad you all approve of my relationship that is none of your business!' says Alex jokingly.

'What about me? Do people not like me?' asks Steph, pouting.

'Of course, everyone loves you, too, Steph! You are definitely invited to the next family party!' Lauren replies.

'Ahh, thanks!'

'What's your plan for the rest of the day then, guys?' asks Lauren.

'Going home to lie on the sofa, watch TV and not move,' replies Steph.

'I don't think we've decided yet. Shall we go and grab your things and decide?' Alex asks me.

'Yeah sure,' I reply.

As I get up from the sofa and walk to the stairs, I hear Steph whispering not quietly enough, 'Is that code for more hanky-panky?'

'Oh, Alex, be a darl and strip the bed, won't you!' calls Lauren.

We go into the bedroom and shake our heads. 'Those two are so embarrassing!' I say to Alex.

'I know. It's just not right talking about stuff like that with your sibling! It's nice we've mended our bridges, though.'

'Yes, it's brilliant you're talking again. Your mum and dad are cool. I know you probably didn't want to do the whole meet the parents thing yet, early days, I know. But as I've met yours, and while we're here...what do you say to meeting mine?'

'Sure, I'd love to. We've already had a little chat on the phone. They seem really nice.'

'Great, shall we get Steph to drop us round?'

'Yeah. Shall we spend the night with them and get a flight back tomorrow?'

'Sounds like a plan. I think they'd like that.'

'So...are they in now...or at work?' he asks, pulling me close.

'They'll be in. They're both retired.'

'In that case, get back in that bed before I strip it!'

Steph pulls up outside Mum and Dad's and gets out of the car. 'Good luck in there, you two!' Alex's face looks worried. 'Not that you'll need it! Sue and Jim are cool!' she adds, hugging him. 'So, are you going to say goodbye to me before you go or is this goodbye again for a bit?' she asks, holding my hands.

'I'll give you a call later. We're going to try and get a flight back tomorrow, though.'

'OK, well in case I don't see you, give me a big squeeze!'

'Thanks for dropping us back, and thanks for helping to fix things with Alex.'

'Any time. You two belong together.'

I kiss her on the cheek and make my way down the path to the house. Alex is carrying my case for me, his rucksack over his shoulder. I'm searching my bag for my keys. It's been so long since I used them, I can't remember which 'safe' compartment I put them in.

The door opens and it's Mum. 'Amy! What are you doing back? Oh, hi! You must be Alex! Come in, come in!' she says, pulling the door open wide.

'Hi, Mum. Yes, this is Alex,' I say, giving her a kiss on the cheek and moving down the hall to let Alex in.

'Hi, Mrs Dixon. Erm, Sue?'

'Yes, please call me Sue! I've told you before! Come here and give me hug!' He puts down my case and bends down to hug Mum. She looks over his shoulder at me and mouths, 'He's lovely!'

I carry on through to the kitchen to greet Dad. He gets up from table. 'Amy! Wasn't expecting you back so soon? Everything OK with lover boy, is it?'

'Dad! Yes, Alex is here!' I point down the hallway where Mum is only just loosening him from her hug.

'Oh, you've both come to visit! I see. Cuppa, love?'

'Yes, please, Dad. Alex, do you want a tea?'

'I'd love a cup, thanks, Jim!' Alex offers his hand to my dad.

He turns around after popping the kettle on, takes his hand in his and shakes it firmly, giving him the 'this is my daughter, so you'd better not mess her about' glare over his glasses. 'Nice to meet you, Alex,' he says, releasing his hand.

'Likewise!' says Alex, looking slightly uncomfortable.

'Please sit, you're making the place look untidy!' says Mum. We all take a seat at the kitchen table. 'So, what brings you both back here?' she asks. 'Not that it's not lovely to see you both!' she adds quickly.

'We just had a work do to go to last night,' I say. There's no need to fill them in on all the dramatics.

'Oh, how lovely. You could have stayed here, you know.'

'Well, we stayed at Lauren's last night, Alex's sister, but we thought we might stay here tonight with you and head back tomorrow?'

'Oh, that's brilliant! We'd love to have you both here. Wouldn't we, Jim?'

'Yeah, shall we go to The Bull for tea, then?' asks Dad, hopeful.

'Yeah, that sounds nice. What do you think, Amy?' Mum looks at me.

'It's fine by me if Alex doesn't mind. It's only cheap pub grub, not the culinary delights you've been treating me to, I'm afraid!'

'Pub grub sounds great to me!' says Alex, and I notice Dad pat him on the shoulder in approval with a big smile on his face as he hands him his cup of tea. Any excuse to go to the pub and Dad's happy!

'You've got a lovely colour on you, love!' says Mum. Mum speak for 'great tan'.

'Thanks!' I say, taking my tea from Dad. Nobody makes a better cup of tea than my dad; he knows exactly how I like it.

'You can get a tan when you come and stay with us, Sue!' says Alex.

'Be careful! Keep saying things like that and we might just take you up on that offer!' says Mum, tapping his hand.

'Well, it's a genuine invite – you're supposed to take us up on the offer. Honestly, you are welcome. Just book your flights. There's plenty of room!'

'Thank you, Alex, that's very generous, but we wouldn't want to get on top of you.'

'Mum, the place is huge! Here, I'll show you some pictures!' I pull out my phone and scroll through a few pictures of the villa, careful not to show her any of our drunken debauchery.

'Wow, that place *is* huge! Look, Jim!'

I turn the phone to show Dad – again, careful not to run into the photos where we're dancing half naked in the swimming pool.

'Yeah, that's a very nice place you have there, Alex. What is it you do for a living again?'

'I'm in property investment and redevelopment, but that place belongs to my parents. It's used for the whole family to book out whenever they want. As my work is there currently, it's kind of my main home.'

'You're extremely lucky. I can see why you didn't want to come back, Amy,' says Dad.

'I take it your suitcase is full of dirty washing?' Mum asks, looking at me.

'Erm, well it is. But I can wash them when we get back. It's fine.'

'It's no bother. Give it here. I'll soon have it all washed and ironed for you!'

Bless her. She's a good 'un, my mum.

CHAPTER TWENTY-FIVE

We've spent the day lounging around with my parents. Alex has bonded with my dad over motorsport and boxing, and with Mum over cooking. I didn't even know he knew so much about these things, but I'm glad he's found some common ground with them. My dad's certainly not the easiest to have a conversation with when it's someone he doesn't know. I think it's done me good having some space from Mum and Dad. I'm too old to be living under their roof now. They used to drive me crazy, but I've really enjoyed spending time with them today.

I'm getting ready to go down the pub; Alex is in the shower. It feels nice to be wearing jeans for a change rather than a summer dress. I look through my wardrobe trying to decide what to wear with them. I want to look casual, but nice. I find a silver chiffon layered vest top and try it on. That'll do, with a pair of heeled boots. Can't be wearing open-toe shoes in this drizzle. I put a few curls through my hair to try and bring some life back into it. I know we're only going down to The Bull, but still, I want to look nice for Alex. I would have made an effort with my appearance to go to the pub pre-Danny anyway. God, Danny. It all seems so long ago.

I'm in the middle of my make-up when Alex walks into my bedroom with a towel wrapped around his waist. 'Oh, hello!' I say to his reflection in my vanity mirror.

'Sorry I took so long. The shower kept going cold!'

'Oh yeah, I'll bet that's Mum downstairs. She doesn't get the concept of not turning the taps on while people are in the shower!'

'You look fantastic!' he says, pulling off his towel and drying himself.

'You don't look too bad yourself!' I reply, eyeing him up in the mirror and biting my lip.

'Oh, you think we've got time to er…?'

'No! Absolutely not while Mum and Dad are up! You'll have to wait until later!' I reluctantly peel my eyes away and get back to the task in hand: Smokey eyes done to the best of my ability… I can never do it as good as Steph. A bit of lippy and I'm good to go. 'Maybe I should invite Steph to the pub?'

'Yeah, why not. It takes some of the pressure off me!' he says, pulling on a pair of jeans and a tight black Armani T-shirt.

'I've never seen you in jeans.' I swivel around to face him. 'Looking hot!' I stand up and put my arms around him.

'Ditto,' he says, holding me around the waist, his hands slipping down to my arse. I tap his hand away in a mock telling off. 'Sorry, your ass just looks so good in these jeans,' he says, kissing me.

I get caught in the moment and forget we're in Mum and Dad's house and that we're on our way out until there's a knock on the door. 'Shit!' We pull away from each other. 'Yes?'

'You pair nearly ready?' asks Mum.

'Yeah! Be down in a minute!'

'OK, love.'

Alex gives me a look that lets me know that he's as gutted as I am to pause what we started.

'Later,' I whisper in his ear and nibble it before leaving him alone in my bedroom. He won't be able to come downstairs for at least five minutes…I giggle. I then text Steph: *Going to The Bull for dinner with the 'rents & Alex. Fancy coming with? xx.*

Mum and Dad are sat at the kitchen table in their jackets and shoes waiting to go. 'How long does it take a bloke to get ready?' grumbles Dad.

'Well, if Mum didn't keep putting the taps on and making his shower go cold, maybe he'd have been ready sooner!'

'Oh, sorry about that. I always forget!'

'It's fine, don't worry. I've invited Steph by the way. Hope that's OK?'

'You know Stephanie is always welcome. Like two peas in a pod, you pair.'

A text comes through. It's Steph: *Sure, as long as you don't mind me gatecrashing your little family partaaay! Could really do with more food. See you in 10? xx.* I reply back, *You know you're welcome! See you in 10 xx.*

It feels great to be walking into the pub hand in hand with Alex. Dad tells us to find a table and that he'll get the drinks. An excuse for him to chat to his mates at the bar. We won't see him for another twenty minutes.

'Fancy sharing a bottle of Pinot Grigio, Mum?'

'Yes, that sounds lovely, dear. Alex, will you join us on the wine?'

'Or would you rather have a pint?' asks Dad.

Oh, dilemma… Is he going to side with Mum or Dad? He looks at me as if to tell him what to do, but I shrug.

'I'll have a pint of Peroni, Jim. Want me to give you a hand?'

'Yeah, can do.'

I haven't seen Alex with a pint. We've had a few bottles of beer around the pool. He really doesn't strike me as a pint kind of guy. But I'm glad about that. The opposite of Danny. I think he's only having a pint to get in my dad's good books.

Mum and I sit at a table, remove our jackets and instantly start reading the menu.

'He seems nice, Amy. I like him,' says Mum.

'He's really nice, Mum. I'm glad you're getting along. I met his mum and dad last night, actually. They seem really lovely, too.'

'Oh, when do we get to meet them, then?'

'Mum, it's a bit soon! I only met them because they were at the work do.'

'Oh, OK,' she says, deflated.

'I promise you can meet them when it's been a few months. OK?'

'OK. I mean it, though. He really is lovely. I know I said Danny was lovely, but I know he didn't really make you happy. You seem to be glowing around Alex. You have a constant smile on your face, and you can't stop looking at each other. And his arms – they're massive, aren't they! He obviously works out; you'll have to start going to the gym, Amy. You don't want to lose that one!'

'Thanks, Mum! I'm glad you like him, though; it means a lot.'

Dad and Alex come back over with the drinks. Alex instinctively pours our wine and puts it in the cooler before sitting next to Dad and grabbing a menu.

'Thank you, Alex, very chivalrous. Jim would have just handed me the glass and bottle and let me get on with it myself!'

Dad rolls his eyes. 'Decided what you're having?' he asks, to no one in particular, changing the subject. Clever Dad.

'I think I'm going to have the cottage pie. They do a lovely home-made cottage pie here,' says Mum.

'I'll join you with that then, Mum,' I say.

'Is the steak any good?' asks Alex.

'No!' we all chorus.

'That's one thing pubs can never seem to get right. It's always tough as old boots!' says Mum.

'In that case, I think I'll have the classic burger,' says Alex.

'Wise choice,' says Dad. 'I'm gonna have the Tex-Mex burger. No point ordering something I get fed at home! Cottage pie!' he says, shaking his head.

'Hi, guys!' calls Steph, walking over to the table. She gives everyone a kiss on the cheek and sits down next to Mum.

'Want some wine with us, Steph?' asks Mum.

'Sure. Well, I'll have one glass. Driving...got work tomorrow, and I don't think they'll appreciate me calling in sick with a hangover again!'

'You didn't?' says Mum, shocked. 'Won't you get the sack for that?'

'Nah, they're cool, don't stress!'

'I'll get you a glass,' says Alex as he gets up from the table. 'Do you know what you want to eat, Steph, and I can order while I'm up there?'

'Ooh, I'll have the chicken salad please, babe, and a side of sweet potato fries!'

'No worries.' He walks over to the bar, and Dad suddenly gets up and chases after him. I'm assuming Mum gave him the 'you're not going to let him pay, are you?' stare. I giggle. So predictable, my parents.

We've all finished our food, Mum and I are halfway through our second bottle of Pinot, and Steph has embarrassed me in front of Mum and Dad by explaining how we met Alex. She knew better than to go any further than that though, thankfully. My mum did laugh, to be fair; but my dad looked horrified! We've filled them in on our encounter with the sea lion and dolphins, and our romantic champagne picnic. Mum made Alex promise to book her in for the dolphin swim when they visit as soon as she realised that she gets a life jacket and no actual swimming is involved. Not a strong swimmer, my mum.

'Anyone for dessert?' asks Dad.

We all shake our heads and exclaim that we're too full up – much to my dad's dismay. He won't order one just for himself. 'I'll go get another pint, then. Pint, Alex?'

'I'm good thanks, Jim,' he says, pointing to the full pint of Peroni still sat in front of him.

'Amy?' I look up and see Danny. Crap.

'Hi. What are you doing in here?'

'Just in for a couple of pints, you know. What are you doing in here? You look great! Really brown?'

'It's called a suntan, Danny,' Steph chimes in sarcastically. 'Oh, Alex, meet Danny. Danny meet Alex!' says Steph, looking gleeful.

I glare at her. Mum sits there as though she's watching her favourite soap, not saying a word.

Alex stands up to shake Danny's hand, and I'm guessing to show how much taller and stronger he is.

'Hi, are you Steph's fella?' asks Danny. Dumbass.

'No. I'm Amy's boyfriend.'

Danny's mouth drops open, and he looks at me and closes it again.

'Did you want something?' I ask him.

'I just came over to say hello...' He starts to walk away but then spins back around. 'How can you have a *boyfriend* already, Amy?'

'What do you mean *already*? You cheated on me with someone else! You had a new girlfriend before you even had the decency to finish with me! Come to think of it, why aren't you in fancy London now with your fancy new woman?'

Alex is still standing, his jaw clenching, his eyes flicking back and forth between me and Danny, waiting for me to give permission to knock him the fuck out.

Danny looks all sheepish. 'It didn't work out. I'm back. That's not the point. You were supposed to *love* me. And you're with someone else already, like a little slut!' I realise he's drunk.

'Excuse me, young man! Nobody calls my daughter that word!' shouts my dad, but before he's finished the sentence, Alex has him pinned to a pillar by his shoulders.

'I think you need to say sorry, Danny. To Amy, and her parents.'

'I'm sorry!' says Danny.

I think he's realised he's not going to win this one. He actually looks like he might cry. If I didn't hate him so much, I might actually feel sorry for him.

'Now, I'm going to let you go, and you're going to be on your way, OK?' says Alex.

'Whatever,' Danny mutters.

'*Whatever* is not going to be good enough, Danny. I need you to confirm that you're going to go home, sober up and not bother Amy again. OK?'

I can see he's trying his best not to show the anger that's obviously bubbling inside him.

'OK,' Danny mumbles, admitting defeat.

Alex lets go, and Danny runs out of the pub.

The pub regulars cheer and clap, blatantly half-cut themselves. Steph joins in, she's not drunk…she's just crazy.

My dad shakes Alex's hand and goes back to the bar to retrieve his pint.

Alex comes over to check on me. 'Are you OK?'

'I am now. Thank you.'

'So, that's he who shan't be named whose name begins with D, huh?'

'That's the one!'

'And the only, I hope?' He tilts up my chin with his finger and kisses me softly. 'I thought I was done fighting men off to get you. Apparently not.'

'Trust me, you have me! He who…oh…Danny…he's history.'

'Glad to hear it.'

'Are you two rejoining the table?' shouts Steph.

We're leaving the pub after staying there for another hour drinking following all the drama with Danny. My dad was so proud of how Alex handled things; he hasn't shut up about it.

'Have a safe flight back, you guys! And, Ames, try and stay out of trouble, hey? Give that man of yours a break!' says Steph.

'Ha, yeah, I'll try!' I say, giving her a big hug.

'Aw, you're wearing the bangle!'

'Of course. I haven't taken it off since you gave it to me!'

'I'll miss ya, beaut, but I'll come and see you in a few months. OK?'

'Course, I look forward to it.'

She says goodbye to everyone else and gets in her car. We start walking home. Alex is straight by my side holding my hand. I even notice that Mum and Dad are holding hands, walking in front. Aww!

'I think my dad loves you,' I say, squeezing Alex's hand.

'I'm doing something wrong if I've got your dad to love me

before you do,' he says casually.

My heart pounds. Maybe he's just joking. I feel like I'm ready to say it, but I don't want to say it and ruin everything. Although I'm already living with the man, things are not very normal in this relationship.

'You OK?' he asks.

'Yeah, sorry. Deep in thought.'

'I've booked our flight home for tomorrow midday. Is that OK?'

'Home?'

'Yeah. What's wrong?'

'Nothing. It just feels weird to call it home, I guess!'

'You do want it to be your home, don't you?' he asks, stopping.

'Absolutely!'

'Good. I thought I was losing you again for a minute there.'

'Alex, I'm sorry for running out on you, but I thought it was for a good reason. Unless you make me, I won't run out on you again.'

'Is that a promise?'

'That's a promise.' I pull his face down to me and kiss him, and the heavens open. I feel glued to the spot. There's something really sexy about kissing in a downpour – not that I've ever done it before.

'Come on, you two!' shouts Mum. 'You'll catch your death!'

We giggle and run to catch them up. We all pile into the house and remove our wet jackets and shoes.

'Do you want another drink, Alex?' calls Dad from the kitchen.

I shake my head with eyebrows raised to the stairs.

'No thanks, Jim, we're tired. I think we're going to call it a night!'

'Suit yourselves!'

'Night, Mum. Night, Dad!' I shout, chasing him up the stairs.

CHAPTER TWENTY-SIX

It feels weird waking up in my old room with Alex next to me. I prop my head up with my elbow and watch him sleep. He is even gorgeous when he's sleeping. And that stuff with Danny last night – that was bloody awesome! He dumps me for some slag in London, and it turns out to be the best thing that ever happened to me. Now Danny's all alone, and he got to see me with my new super-hot, super-strong boyfriend. It's kinda perfect actually.

Alex opens his eyes and smiles. 'Morning, beautiful.'

'Morning.' I smile back.

'Last night was kind of hot, in a weird way, wasn't it...trying to be quiet!'

'Yes, it was! We could hardly move without the bed squeaking, but it just made it more intense somehow!'

'You are so amazing, Amy. I feel like our bodies are so in tune with each other. Does that make me sound corny?'

'No, not at all. I feel it, too. It's like we were made for each other.'

'Yes, like soulmates.'

'Like soulmates.' I nod. 'OK, that might be a little corny!' I laugh. 'Wanna try and not make any noise again?'

'Hell yeah!' Alex rolls me over on top of him, and I giggle. 'Shhh!' he whispers.

The way he makes me feel is so incredible. It is as though we were made for each other. Even in between the giggling and the shushing, my body doesn't get distracted.

Afterwards, I lie on top of him breathless. 'I love you,' I whisper, feeling magnificent. I open my eyes in a panic. Shit. I was not supposed to say that yet. Crap. I lie there in silence; I daren't sit up and look him in the eye. Shit. What if I've gone and ruined it all? It was just in the heat of the moment. It just slipped out. I didn't mean to say it! Well, I do mean it, of course I mean it. He's swept me off my feet. I mean he's everything. Why wouldn't I love him?

He rolls me over so I'm underneath him. I keep my focus on the bedroom door – too afraid to look at him. He moves my head, making me have eye contact. 'I'm not sure if you said what I think you just said? But at the risk of sounding like an idiot...I love you, Amy.'

The biggest smile takes over my worried face and I kiss him. 'I love you, Alex. Promise me you're still not going to turn into a psycho in a few weeks!'

'I promise.' He laughs.

We walk into the kitchen smiling like Cheshire cats. 'Morning, lovebirds,' says Mum. 'Cuppa?'

'Yes please!' I say, cringing and sitting down. God, I hope they didn't hear us.

'Your dad's just popped out to get some sausages. Sausage sarnies OK with you, Alex?'

'Yeah, sounds great. Thanks, Sue.'

'Amy, all your things are washed and ironed and hanging up in my room, ready for you to repack. I didn't want to burst into your room, what with Alex in bed with you.'

'Ah thanks, Mum, you're a superstar!'

'It's no problem. It's nice to do something for you before you disappear again.'

'But you'll be out to visit soon, won't you?' I ask.

'Just as soon as you want us there,' she says, smiling. As she gives us both our tea, Dad walks through the front door.

'Ah, morning, you lazy pair!' he calls while removing his shoes and hanging up his jacket. Dad places a brown paper bag on the table. 'I decided to go to the butchers for the sausages. Did you know they do cooked sarnies? I thought I might as well get them already cooked!'

'Oh, no I didn't know that. It must be a new thing!' Dad hands us each a hot sandwich wrapped in white paper while Mum fetches plates and sauces. 'Thanks, Dad, this is really good!' I must go on a healthy diet and get out of holiday eating mode or Mum's right – I'll need to join a gym. And I don't want to have to do that, if I can help it.

'Alex wouldn't let me pay for dinner, so thought the least I can do is pay for breakfast,' says Dad. 'What time do you need to get going, love?'

'We need to be at the airport in about two hours,' says Alex.

'Want a lift?' asks Dad.

'Yes please, Dad. That'd be great. Actually, you might as well have my car, Mum, while I'm away. I'm not going to be needing it for a while.'

'Oh smashing. Thanks. It's not often we both need to use the car but when we do, it doesn't half cause an argument!'

'It doesn't cause an argument,' says Dad. 'It's just a disagreement.'

'Mmm, well, whatever it is, it'll be nice. Thanks, Amy.'

'That's OK, Mum. I'd better go and pack my things. After a couple of days in the rain, I'm looking forward to getting back to the sun!'

Both Mum and Dad drop us off at the airport. Dad is about to lift my case out of the boot, but Alex quickly takes over and also retrieves his rucksack.

Dad shakes Alex's hand, less aggressively this time, and cups their shaking hands in his other. Smiling, he says, 'Alex, I have no doubt you'll take good care of our Amy. Thank you again for giving that piece of shit Danny what for last night!'

'I promise I'll take the best care of her, Jim,' Alex replies.

Mum gives me a hug. 'Have you got enough money, love?'

'Yeah, I'll be fine thanks. And I'll pay you back everything I used on the travel card as soon I can, I swear!'

'There's no need for that, Amy!'

'No, I know, but I want to pay you back. Maybe I can load the card back up ready for your visit?'

'Well, that'll be nice, but don't leave yourself short doing it!' she says, wagging her finger.

'I won't. Well, I don't actually know what I'm getting paid yet!'

We swap over, and I cuddle Dad while Alex cuddles Mum.

'Bye, Dad.'

'Bye, darling, it was lovely to see you. And I'm very impressed with your new chap.'

'Thanks, Dad, it was great seeing you too. I'll see you soon.'

As we walk away, I look back and wave and see that Dad has his arm around Mum as she sheds a little tear. Bless her. It's been so lovely seeing them, but I am looking forward to getting back to life with Alex now. In the sun.

We enter the airport and check in. Well, I say 'we'. Alex checks in; I'm busy texting everyone on my phone. A quick bye to Steph saying that we'll Skype soon. Then a quick text to Lauren thanking her for everything.

I'm called forward to check my face against my passport, so I throw my phone into my bag and step forward. Free of luggage, we go through security. I walk through smiling – and oh, look at that, I don't need the extra security wand treatment today! I'm waved straight through. We pick up our bags from the scanner and hold hands.

'We're going to this little lounge over here,' says Alex, pointing the way.

'Oh, OK!'

We walk in, and Alex gives his name and shows some sort of card. Then the lady walks us over to this amazing seating area. There are leather sofas, funny little egg-shaped chairs with little tables in front of them, and it's peaceful and quiet. None of the usual mayhem that lies behind the door to the rest of the airport.

'Here's your reserved seating, sir,' says the polite lady who showed us to our seat. She's very smiley and happy, not at all like the staff you get in the Wetherspoons at the airport, who seem harassed and stressed and annoyed that you had the audacity to order a drink! Mind you, I think I'd be annoyed serving drinks to people who are about to go on holiday, too.

Alex thanks the lovely lady and she removes a sign that says 'Reserved for 2 – Stevenson'.

'What is this place?' I ask. 'And how have I never known about it before?'

'It's the business class lounge,' he says.

'Oh, very swanky! No wonder I've never been here before. Does that mean all the food and drink over there is *free*?' I ask, hopeful.

He laughs. 'Yes, it does. What would you like, and I'll get it for you?'

'I think I need to see this for myself. I'll go! You want anything?'

'I'll have a glass of champagne. And just a light snack if you can manage it.'

'Free champagne!' I squeal and march over to check out what's on offer. They've got everything going on in here. Tiny little sandwiches on every bread you can imagine, vol-au-vents, croissants, cakes, even hot stew and mashed potatoes. Blimey! The diet can start tomorrow!

I pick us up a cake each. Even though I really want to try a bit of everything, we didn't have our sausage sarnies that long ago, and I don't want to look greedy. Then I go in search of champagne. There are tea- and coffee-making facilities along with a fridge full of bottled beer and soft drinks. People are just helping themselves. There's a bottle opener hanging from the fridge on a string. Steph would bloody love this place! Then I spot the champagne. Several bottles actually, in a large cooler. I pour us both a glass and then stand there wondering how I'm going to carry a plate with two cakes and two glasses of champers.

'Do you need a hand?' It's the lovely lady who showed us to our seats.

'Oh, yes please! I really didn't think this one through! Thank you so much!'

She picks up both glasses and carries them over for me.

With my free hand, I can't resist adding two of the little sand-wiches that are bursting with egg mayo and cress onto the plate. 'Thanks again,' I say to the lady as she places our drinks down.

'No problem!' She smiles.

I sit down next to Alex. 'This place is so cool!'

He laughs. 'I'm glad you like it!'

'It's so chilled in here! Not rammed with knobheads, there's free food and booze, and saved seats! I mean, this is just brilliant!'

'I wanted to talk to you about something, while we have some quiet, and before you take full advantage of the free champagne!'

'OK?' I sip my drink. It's delicious; he's right. I need to down this and take full advantage. With any luck, it'll knock me out for the whole plane journey again.

'I wanted to talk to you about these.' He produces a notepad from his bag and flicks to the sketches I drew at Prego.

'Oh, I was just doodling...you know... If you don't like them, that's fine, I can redo it... I just had things come to mind so wanted to jot them down while I remembered.'

He puts a finger on my lips to shush me. 'Stop, Amy. You're rambling again! I think they're really good! Excellent, in fact.'

'You do? Oh, I'm so pleased!'

'Yes, I do. And I think if you can do some larger sketches like this, we can present them to the manager at Prego. I think he will love them, and then he'll embrace the change. He's a bit of a stubborn old mule; he takes a bit of convincing. But this, I just know *this* will do it. *You* will do it.'

'Thanks! I mean, if you think so. I'd love to!'

'And your pay is going to match your talent, don't you worry about that. I'll make sure you're on a top salary.'

'Thank you, Alex. I'm really excited to get started on it.'

'Good. Well, you can get started tomorrow. Let's enjoy what we have left of today.' He necks his champagne. 'Another?'

I down mine to catch up. 'Is the Pope Catholic?'

We board the plane before anyone else. I've never done that before. I'm usually amongst the last passengers to be called in the cheap seats...with the cattle, as my dad says. Come to think of it, I've never flown with British Airways before. I'm always on a low-budget airline like Ryanair or EasyJet.

Alex sits on this large blue leather luxury chair, which has a ton of leg room and a packet of goodies on the seat.

'Is this business class?' I ask.

'Yeah. Well, you know, we're flying for business, aren't we? I can put this through expenses.'

'Wow. I've never even seen business class before!' I reply.

I settle into my seat, which is so comfy. Oh yeah, I can sleep the whole journey in this bad boy! I rummage through my goody bag. A pen, toothbrush and toothpaste, and an eye mask – awesome! That is going to make my plane nap even better. Socks...? Why would I need socks? That's a bit random. Earplugs – another thing that will aid my sleep.

After taking a look around, I see that there's hardly anyone sat in this section. Then everyone else begins to file on, giving us death stares as they walk past to get to their crummy economy-class seats. I feel a bit guilty, but I don't know why – that would normally be me!

I lean over and whisper to Alex, 'Don't you think it's a bit cruel that they put economy class at the back, and then make everyone walk through the nice bit to see what they're missing out on? Have a look at what you could have won!'

'I suppose, yeah. Is it that bad in the back?'

'Have you never flown economy?' I ask, astonished.

'When I was younger, I think, but I don't really remember it.'

'Lucky you!'

'We can fly your mum and dad out business class when they visit.'

'Really? They would love that! They're really taken with you.

My big macho man who protects me.'

'And are *you*?'

'You know I am!'

'Because I meant what I said this morning. I don't know if you just said it in the heat of the moment, and maybe you've been kicking yourself ever since, but I meant it. I love you, Amy.'

'I totally meant it! I love you, too, Alex, and I feel like the luckiest girl in the world.' I sit back and look at the gorgeous man next to me, who loves me, who protects me. And it's true. I am the luckiest girl in the world.

THE END

ACKNOWLEDGEMENTS

I have thoroughly enjoyed writing my first book! It wouldn't have been possible without some incredible people in my life. Firstly, the support of my husband Don, thank you so much for putting up with me ignoring you all night, and all your soppy 'I'm proud of you' moments. My bestie Mel, thank you for being the first one to read my first few chapters and for giving me the reassurance I needed to continue. Mel, Leya & Kathy you all read my first draft, and your positivity and praise about my book on this journey have been so encouraging. Thank you so much. Love you guys! Also, my very talented brother Rob, for creating my excellent book cover. You've done a fantastic job of it, (credits to Leya for the design ideas and Mom for the advice and input). It's perfect, thank you – or should I say, 'Nice One Bruvvaaaa!' And last but not least, I'd like to thank Alex. Not the heartthrob character in my book, but my amazing editor. Thank you so much for all your hard work and making my novel complete. You also had many kind, heartening words to say about my writing, and coming from an editor on my first attempt at a book, it was greatly received.

ABOUT THE AUTHOR

Linsey Cross is a mother of two young children and working a full-time job in the telecoms industry, whist writing stories at night, with much patience from her husband. When not working or writing, she is usually on holiday, booking her next holiday, or dreaming about her next holiday.

To find out more about Linsey, and to find out any updates on upcoming novels, like her Facebook page: https://www.facebook.com/linseyjcross/

Printed in Great Britain
by Amazon